HER SURRENDER

ANNA STONE

CHAPTER ONE

"*I* can't believe she broke up with me over text." April scowled and placed her phone on the table next to her plate. "Who does that?"

"That's pretty cold," Lexi said between mouthfuls. "Did she say why?"

"No, but I have a few ideas." Actually, it was more like a long list of ideas. At the very top of it was the fact that April and Christie had fought constantly. "We were only together for six weeks, but the least she could do was call me!"

"No one makes phone calls anymore." Lexi pushed one of her dark curls out of her face. "At least she didn't just ghost you."

"You're not helping, Lex." April's long-time friend and coworker had a cavalier attitude when it came to relationships.

"Sorry," Lexi replied. "I know it sucks, but just last week you were saying that you weren't that into her. Admit it, you were going to break up with her anyway."

"*If* I was going to break up with her, I would have done it in person."

"Look at it this way. She saved you the trouble of an uncomfortable conversation."

"I guess." April rested her chin on her hand. "I'm never getting back that book I lent her, am I?"

"Probably not," Lexi shoveled the last of her lunch into her mouth.

April wasn't that upset, not really. Christie had been nice, and they had a lot in common, but there were no sparks between them. What bothered April was that this was just the latest in a string of short relationships that had fizzled out, mostly because of personality clashes. April, as one of her exes put it, was "strong-willed". She was pretty sure that meant that she was hard to get along with.

April sighed. She was twenty-eight now. She knew that it was silly, but she was beginning to feel like she was doomed to spend the rest of her life alone. All her friends were pairing off and getting married, then moving away to start new lives, and April was being left behind.

"We should head back," April said. Their lunch hour was almost over.

"Yes, boss," Lexi said.

Waving goodbye to the cook, April and Lexi left the diner. It was a short walk from the library where they both worked, so they went there regularly for lunch. The diner had been there for as long as April could remember, and it was one of the few remaining local, family-run businesses in the area. But with rent prices going up as they were, April wondered how much longer the diner would last.

April and Lexi made their way back to work, chatting as

they walked. Their workplace, the Oakmont Street Library, was just a few blocks away. The library was more than a library. It doubled as a community center and a meeting place for everyone who lived in this part of the city.

April was the library's director, but only for the last few months. She'd worked at the library for years and had been promoted to the top spot after the old director's sudden resignation. The timing couldn't have been worse. As soon as April had taken over, all of Oakmont Street, including the library and the surrounding apartments, had been bought by a multinational property development company. Oasis Developments had big plans for Oakmont Street. And those plans didn't involve leaving the library standing.

Lexi and April reached the library and headed to their small shared office in the back. Lexi was the library's event coordinator, which had been April's position before her promotion. The two of them, along with a few others, made up a bare-bones staff that barely kept the place running. Somehow, the library scraped by despite all the funding cuts.

But now, its time was running out.

April picked up the bundle of mail that had been left on her desk and flicked through it. She reached an envelope with a familiar logo. Her heart stopped.

It was a letter from Oasis Developments.

Ever since Oasis bought the building, April had been trying to get in touch with them to talk about the library, but all of her phone calls and emails had been ignored. This was the only piece of correspondence the library had received from Oasis in months.

April ripped open the letter and scanned the page. Her stomach sank.

"Everything okay, April?" Lexi asked.

"It's from Oasis. We have 90 days to vacate the building." April collapsed into her chair. She'd known this was coming since Oasis bought the building. The city didn't have the funds to relocate the library, so they were on their own. Unless April could come up with a way to save it, the library would be forced to close its doors. "It's official. This is really happening."

Lexi placed a hand on April's arm. "Sorry, April. I know how much this place means to you."

The library was special to April, for reasons that ran deeper than the fact that she worked here. It was *her* library. She'd always thought of it as hers, even before she became director, even before she started working here as a page in high school.

"They can't just tear it down," April said. "Half of West Heights has already been torn down by developers. Soon there's not going to be anything left." April dropped the letter onto her desk. "It feels like everything is changing so fast, and there's nothing I can do to stop it."

"I know," Lexi said. "It sucks."

April sighed.

"Do you know what would cheer you up?"

April raised an eyebrow. "Does it involve getting drunk?" That was usually Lexi's go-to suggestion.

"No," Lexi said, feigning offense. "Well, yes, it involves alcohol, but that's not the point." She sat down in her chair and rolled it over to April's desk. "Come to The Sapphire Room with me tonight."

April groaned. The Sapphire Room was the city's lesbian bar. April hadn't been there in years. Lexi, however, went there on a regular basis, usually to pick up women.

"Come on," Lexi said. "It'll be fun. And you never know, you might meet someone."

"I've had enough of relationships for a while. I'm not looking to start another."

"Who said anything about a relationship?" Lexi asked. "Nothing like a mindless one-night stand to help you forget about all your problems."

"I don't know," April said. "That's not my thing."

"Come on, it'll be fun. I'll be your wing-woman."

"I guarantee that you'll be the one dragging some woman home with you within an hour."

"Then you won't have to stay for long, will you?" Lexi said. "Just a few drinks. If you're not having fun, you can go home."

"All right," April said. "Just a few drinks."

April leaned back against the bar, sipping the mojito she'd been nursing since they arrived. It was loaded with sugar, probably to mask the taste of the cheap rum.

As soon as she'd walked through the door, April remembered why she hadn't been to The Sapphire Room in years. The bar, which was decorated in an eclectic mix of shabby chic styles, was too loud, and much too crowded.

"Anyone catch your eye yet?" Lexi asked, scanning the crowd.

"Not really," April replied.

They'd been here for almost an hour, drinking and chatting. Lexi was making a valiant effort to stay with April, but April could tell that her friend was losing her resolve with every woman who shot her a flirtatious glance. April didn't understand why, but women practically threw themselves at Lexi. She seemed to be seeing a different woman every week. To her credit, Lexi was always upfront with the women she met about her casual approach when it came to dating. It didn't deter them.

"You know, you'd have more luck if you didn't glower at every woman who looks your way," Lexi said.

"I am *not* glowering." Nevertheless, April tried to look more relaxed. "It doesn't matter. I'm not interested in anyone anyway."

"It might help you get over Christie," Lexi said.

"Is sex your solution to all of life's problems?"

"Not all of them. Just most of them. Besides, I seem to remember you complaining about how boring your sex life was even when you were with Christie. When was the last time you actually had good sex?"

"God, I can't even remember." April's last few relationships had lacked any excitement in bed. Pretty much every part of her life was lacking in excitement right now.

Lexi shook her head. "Life is too short for bad sex. Or worse—no sex." She downed the rest of her beer. "I'm going to the ladies' room, I'll be right back."

"Okay."

April placed her drink on the bar and pulled down the hem of her dress. She didn't know why she'd bothered to dress up. It wasn't like she was trying to impress anyone.

Her mind wandered back to the library. There were

ninety days until the library had to close its doors. Ninety days to come up with a way to save it. April spent the next few minutes brainstorming ideas but came up empty.

When Lexi returned, she had a guilty look on her face. "So, I know I kind of forced you to come here…"

"Seriously?" April said. "You're going home with someone?"

"*Someone* is coming home with me. I hate sleeping in another woman's bed."

"How did you meet someone in the five minutes you were gone?"

Lexi shrugged. "There was a line for the bathroom. I started talking to the woman in front of me. We had a very interesting conversation." Lexi cocked her head toward a gorgeous long-haired woman standing near the door, typing away on her phone. She was exactly Lexi's type.

"I'm sure it was her conversation that won you over," April said. "It's okay, I was getting bored anyway. I'll probably just go home. Have fun."

"Have I ever told you that you're an amazing friend?"

"Only every time something like this happens."

Lexi grinned. "I'll see you on Monday."

April watched Lexi walk over to the woman, smoothly slide her arm around the woman's waist, and lead her out the door. April finished off the last of her drink. If she left now, she could be in bed by eleven-thirty. Perhaps a good night's sleep would help her tackle her problems in the morning.

As April turned to leave, she noticed a woman standing at the other end of the bar, waiting to order a drink. She looked older than April, but not by much. She was tall and slender, with high cheekbones, and short, feathery blonde hair that was swept back from her face. She was dressed in a way that seemed effortless and stylish at the same time. Dark skinny jeans. A black blazer with the sleeves rolled up. Heeled ankle boots. She possessed an androgynous air while still seeming utterly feminine.

Had the woman been here all along? The bar was small, and April had been idly watching the crowd all night. April definitely would have noticed someone like her. She simply radiated this cool confidence that made it impossible for April to tear her eyes away.

Suddenly, the woman turned toward her. Her eyes locked onto April's across the bar. The woman smiled, an enchanting smile that made April's whole body weak. A smile that whispered a suggestion into April's ear.

April looked away, her heart racing. The woman at the other end of the bar had turned April's legs to jelly with no more than a look. What could she do with a word?

A touch?

April's skin grew hot. She had barely shared a glance with this woman, yet her mind was going off to indecent places. What was wrong with her? It was time for her to get out of here. She fished around in her purse, looking for her phone so she could order a ride.

"Hi."

April looked up. The woman was standing right next to her.

"My name is Victoria." She smiled. "But you can call me Vicki."

CHAPTER TWO

"*A*nd you are?" Vicki asked.

Where did she come from? April had been so lost in her head that the slim blonde had seemed to materialize next to her.

"April," she stammered. April, tongue-tied over a woman? If Lexi could see her right now, she'd have a field day.

"What are you drinking, April?" Vicki had to lean in so that April could hear her voice over the noise of the bar.

"A mojito," April replied.

Vicki waved over the bartender. "Two mojitos."

Wait, what? This woman was buying April a drink now? This wasn't part of the plan. April was supposed to be going home.

Vicki turned back to April. "Did that friend of yours abandon you?"

April nodded. "She picked up someone in the bathroom," she said, finally regaining the ability to speak in full sentences. Wait, how long had Vicki been watching her?

"I'm glad she did," Vicki said. "I've been waiting to get you alone."

"And why is that?" April's wits were returning now. And suddenly, Vicki's smile seemed more arrogant than alluring.

"I wanted to talk to you," Vicki replied.

"About what?"

"How about we start with why you're here tonight?"

"I'm here because my friend dragged me along with her," April said. "But since she's gone, I was planning to go home."

"Was? Does that mean you're not planning to go home anymore?"

April hesitated. "That depends if I can find a reason to stay."

"Here's one right now." Vicki tilted her head in the direction of the bartender. She'd just finished making their drinks. She placed them on the bar in front of them. Vicki slid one of the glasses over to April. "Now you have a reason."

April picked up the drink and sipped it nonchalantly. She didn't want Vicki to think she was interested. Because she wasn't. Even if she was, it was only because Vicki was outrageously attractive. Those cheekbones of hers could cut glass, and her eyes were a striking green. And she was so tall; although, everyone was tall compared to April.

Everything about Vicki seemed too perfect. Even though her outfit was casual, her clothes were fine, almost too nice for a place like this. And she smelled divine, a sweet, citrusy scent that could only have come from a very expensive bottle.

April realized that neither of them had spoken in a while. "Why are you here tonight?" she shot back.

"I was hoping someone exceptional would walk through the door." Vicki ran her fingers through her short hair. "I'd given up until I saw you."

If those words had come out of anyone else's mouth, April would have rolled her eyes and walked away. But somehow, coming from Vicki's lips, they made April want to melt.

"Judging by the way you were looking at me earlier, you were thinking the same thing," Vicki said, never taking her eyes off April's.

"Can't a girl just admire the view?" April asked.

"You're admitting it then? That you were checking me out?"

"I didn't say that," April said, twirling a lock of her long brown hair around her finger. When she realized what her hands were doing, she stopped. She was not some flirting teenage girl.

"You never did answer my question." Vicki leaned down on the bar. "Why did you really come here tonight? It can't be just because of your friend."

"Do I need a reason to come to a bar? Maybe I just wanted a drink."

"You're not here to drink. You can't have had more than a couple of drinks, or you'd be at least tipsy. And you're not the type to come to a place like Sapphire for no reason."

"How do you know that?"

"I can tell," Vicki said. "And, I would have seen you here before if you were."

"Spend a lot of time here hitting on women, do you?"

April had been friends with Lexi for years. She knew a player when she saw one.

Vicki placed her glass down on the bar. "It's my turn to ask questions."

"Excuse me?"

"You heard what I said," Vicki replied. "But since you don't seem inclined to answer me, I'm going to make an educated guess."

April crossed her arms. "Go ahead."

"You're here to take your mind off your problems."

April shrugged. "Maybe."

"And what would those problems be?"

"The usual. Work. Women. Everything."

"I can't imagine you having problems with women," Vicki said.

"Are you kidding?" April said. "I have nothing but problems with women. And it's not like they're lining up to date me."

"Of course they're not. They're all intimidated by you."

"*I'm* intimidating?"

"Extremely," Vicki replied. "Not to mention you're the hottest woman in the room. That's intimidating."

"That didn't stop you."

"Because I like a challenge."

April shook her head. "It's a game to you? Finding a woman at a bar and seeing if you can get her to go home with you?"

"I do enjoy playing games," Vicki said. "But that part comes later."

April gaped at her. What exactly was Vicki suggesting? A number of naughty images sprang up in April's mind.

"How about we ditch this bar and go somewhere nicer?" Vicki asked.

April narrowed her eyes. "Somewhere nicer?"

"Yes. A different bar, for example."

"I'm sure that's what you meant."

"Why, did you have somewhere else in mind?" Vicki propped her elbow up on the bar and crossed her ankles. "I'm open to suggestions."

April couldn't believe Vicki's nerve. Did she really think that it was a given that April would go home with her? That as soon as they stepped through the door Vicki would have April up against the wall and begging for Vicki to…

Wow. Where had that thought even come from?

"So, what do you say?" Vicki asked.

April bit the inside of her cheek. Her mind was telling her to put her drink down, and walk out the door, to go home to the comfort of her bed. But the rest of her body was screaming something completely different.

"I know what you're doing. You're trying to find an excuse to walk away. You're telling yourself that you shouldn't do this, you shouldn't want this." Vicki leaned in closer. "It's only one night. Give in to temptation just this once."

There was something hypnotic about Vicki's smooth voice, and her perfect skin, and her dark green eyes. They seemed so endless, so easy to get lost in.

Or maybe those mojitos were stronger than April realized.

Vicki straightened up. "Of course, if you're not interested, just say the word and I'll leave you alone."

Vicki drummed her fingers on the bar next to her. With

every tap, April could feel her reservations falling away. Her eyes wandered down to Vicki's full, coral red lips...

"Kiss me," she said.

"What?" For the first time that night, Vicki's composed facade wavered.

"Kiss me." April gave Vicki a tantalizing smile. "I want to know what I'm getting myself into."

Something ignited in Vicki's eyes. Without hesitation, she reached out and cupped April's cheek in her hand, drawing her into a searing hot kiss.

At once, April crumbled. She closed her eyes and let Vicki's mint-tinged lips and heady scent overwhelm her senses. Her head began to spin, and the floor seemed to slip out from under her.

April pulled back, breathless. "Okay."

"Okay, what?" Vicki asked.

"Okay. I'll come home with you." It was just one night after all. One night, no strings. And April was going to keep her head.

Not five minutes later, they were in the back seat of a cab on the way to Vicki's apartment, their lips and arms locked together in a tempest of lust.

April and Vicki walked down the hall to Vicki's apartment. They had ended up in a nice part of the city, in a fancy apartment building. April didn't have a chance to comment before Vicki pushed her up against what April hoped was her front door.

April grabbed onto Vicki's waist, pulling her in closer.

Vicki pressed her lips to April's in an insistent kiss. April struggled to keep herself from dissolving into Vicki's skin. She wasn't doing a very good job of keeping her head.

"Mmph." April shoved Vicki away playfully. "Shouldn't we wait until we're inside? Do you really want to give your neighbors a show?"

"They're going to get a show either way," Vicki replied. "The whole building is going to hear us later."

"You're a lot of talk, but I'm not seeing any action."

"Oh, I'm going to make you regret saying that." Vicki unlocked the door. "Inside."

As soon as Vicki opened the door, her expensive clothes and perfume made sense. A place like this, in this part of the city, would cost a fortune. The spacious loft was sleek and open, with high ceilings and big windows. It was all pale wood and glass, clean and white, while still feeling warm and welcoming.

"After you," Vicki said.

April stepped inside. A small black cat stood up on the arm of the couch, yellow eyes glinting in the light. He looked at her and arched his back, his fur standing up, then darted off into the kitchen.

"That's Sebastian," Vicki said, flinging her blazer over the back of a chair. "Ignore him, he gets jealous."

April turned in a circle in the center of the room. "This is a nice place."

Vicki appeared behind her, wrapping her arms around April's waist. She kissed the side of her neck. "If you think this is impressive, you should see the bedroom."

"In a hurry to get me out of this dress, are you?" April asked.

"What can I say? I'm simply dying to see what's underneath it."

"Do your corny lines ever work on anyone?"

"You're standing in my apartment right now, aren't you?" Vicki said, running her fingers through her blonde locks. "You tell me."

God, it was so sexy when she did that. "Show me the way to your bedroom and I'm yours."

Vicki grabbed April's hand and pulled her down the hall and into her bedroom. It looked much the same as the rest of the house, but not as bright. It was decorated in various shades of gray, with hints of red. There was a huge closet built into one wall. Apparently, the stylish woman owned a lot of clothing.

Vicki kicked off her boots. "You have twenty seconds to get out of that dress."

A smile spread on April's lips. She liked a woman who took charge in the bedroom. "Why don't you come here and take it off me?" April asked.

Vicki answered April's challenge by backing her toward the bed, unzipping April's dress, and yanking it over her head in the space of a few seconds.

She pushed April onto the bed and raked her eyes down April's body. "Where have you been all my life, April?"

"Just shut up and get over here," April said.

Vicki raised an eyebrow. "I don't take too kindly to being ordered around."

"What are you going to do about it?" April asked.

Without taking her eyes off April, Vicki stripped off her clothing until she was left in only a pair of black panties. Then she dived onto the bed and tore off April's bra, flinging it to the side, and kissed April greedily. Her hand skimmed down to April's chest, caressing the curves of her breasts and the peaks of her nipples.

April let out a soft murmur, drawing Vicki down to her. Vicki's thigh slipped between April's, pressing against her panty-covered mound. April ran her palms up Vicki's smooth stomach and over her breasts. Above her, Vicki let out a halting breath.

She straightened up, kneeling over April with one leg at either side of her. "Why don't we have a little fun?"

"Oh?" April bit her lip. "What kind of fun."

"Stay right there."

"Yes, ma'am."

Vicki got up and walked over to a chest at the end of the bed. She opened the lid and began to dig through its contents, seemingly searching for something in particular. A toy of some kind? Vicki had mentioned that she liked to play games.

Whatever Vicki was looking for, it was taking far too long. April crawled to the end of the bed and peered into the chest.

"What's… oh!"

Inside the chest was a large collection of toys. Sure, there was a strap-on and a vibrator. But on top of that, there were handcuffs, ropes, a blindfold—even some kind of whip.

Vicki gave April a firm stare. "Didn't I tell you to stay there?"

April frowned. "Yes, but-"

"Then why didn't you?"

"Because I wanted to see what you were doing." April paused. "Is that a whip?"

"It's not a whip," Vicki said. "It's a riding crop."

April raised an eyebrow. "How do you know so much about that?"

"Let's just say what's in this chest isn't even half of my collection."

"Where's the rest of it?"

Vicki shut the lid. "Wouldn't you like to know?"

"Come on," April said. "You can't say something like that and not show me."

"I don't think so. There's a reason I keep it all hidden away. The rest of my collection isn't for the faint of heart."

"I'm no stranger to that kind of thing," April said. "It doesn't scare me."

"Let me guess. Someone tied you to a bed once and now you're an expert in all things kinky?" Vicki said.

April's cheeks grew warm. "Are *you* an expert in all things kinky?"

"You didn't answer my question."

"They were handcuffs. Someone handcuffed me to the bed." It was an old girlfriend of hers, one of her many relationships that didn't last. "It doesn't matter. Nothing that you could show me would shock me."

"I wouldn't be so sure about that," Vicki said.

April folded her arms across her chest. "Try me."

For a split second, Vicki's eyes flicked over to the closet built into the wall.

That was the only hint April needed. She leaped off the bed and made a beeline for the closet. Vicki made a half-hearted attempt to stop her, but not before April reached the closet and flung the doors open.

Her jaw dropped. "What the hell?"

"Do you still think nothing could shock you?" Vicki asked.

April scanned the contents of the enormous closet. It didn't contain clothing. Instead, illuminated by bright lights, were racks and shelves full of every kind of kinky toy imaginable.

Her eyes fell on a series of silver chains, all with different types of clips at the ends. "Are those…"

"Nipple clamps?" Vicki said. "Yes."

April pulled her hand away. Moving on, she ran her hands along a rack of various leather implements. She picked one up, a short black whip with dozens of tails, and held it before her. "Why do you have all this?"

"Because I'm a Domme." Vicki held out her hand and stared at April until she placed the whip in it. She slipped it back into its place on the rack. "I can tell by the look in your eyes that I don't have to explain to you what that means."

April knew what it meant, in a general sense at least. "Do you do this for a living?"

"It's more of a hobby," Vicki replied. "Something I enjoy."

"You get turned on by this?"

"Do you?"

April hesitated. She had never been interested in anything like this. At least, not anything this extreme. But for the past few minutes, the heat between her thighs had been steadily increasing.

"Of course, I enjoy all things vanilla too," Vicki said. "I wouldn't have invited you over if I didn't." She shut the closet doors, hiding everything from view. "Why don't we-"

"Show me." The words flew out of April's mouth before she knew what she was saying.

"Show you what?"

"Show me what you do as a Domme. Show me how you use all of this." April gestured toward the closet.

"Those are just tools. And they're not for beginners." Vicki led her back to the bed and sat down next to her. "Besides, that's not how it works. An interaction between a Domme and her submissive isn't about whips and chains. It goes far deeper than that."

"Then show me what it's really about." April rearranged herself so that she was kneeling on the bed with her legs tucked underneath her. "Please?"

Vicki studied April silently for a moment. "Did you like it?"

"Like what?" April asked.

"Being handcuffed to the bed."

"Yes," April said. The memory of that night had stayed seared in her mind. "I liked it."

"Why?" Vicki asked. "What did you like about it?"

"I'll tell you if you agree to show me what you do."

"I don't make a habit of letting submissives dictate terms."

"Can't you make an exception?"

Vicki searched April's face, her green eyes probing into April's. April held her gaze. She didn't know why, but she wanted this so badly.

Vicki shook her head. "All right," she finally said. "I'll show you."

CHAPTER THREE

"Strip off your panties and come here," Vicki said.

April did as she was told, moving to stand in front of Vicki in the center of the rug. "What are you going to do?" she asked.

"You'll see. Don't worry, I'm not going to use any of my toys."

"Then how are you going to show me what you do?"

Vicki didn't answer her. "You need to choose a safeword. Something you're unlikely to say accidentally."

"Why do I need a safeword if you're not going to use your toys?"

"Safewords aren't just for physical play," Vicki said. "Your safeword?"

April thought for a moment. "Cinnamon."

"Cinnamon it is. Say the word, and everything stops."

April nodded. "Okay."

Almost immediately, there was a subtle shift in Vicki's demeanor. The green in her eyes darkened, and her physical presence grew to fill the room. It was like she slipped on a mask, one that amplified a certain side of her. It was the side of Vicki that had made April fall to pieces the moment their eyes had met in the bar.

"You seem to have this idea that BDSM is all physical," Vicki said. "In reality, it's all in the mind. Everything in my closet? It's all window dressing. I don't need any of it to gain your submission. I'm going to show you that right now."

"How?" April asked.

"I'm going to peel back all your defenses and work my way deep inside you until you're truly vulnerable," Vicki said. "Until you have no choice but to surrender."

A shiver rolled down the back of April's neck. She kept her face blank, not letting Vicki see how much she was getting under her skin.

"And then," Vicki said, a smile playing on her lips, "You're going to beg me for release."

April smirked. "You can try."

"I'm very good at what I do. If I say you're going to beg, then you're going to beg. That brings me to the rules of the game." Vicki began to pace in front of her slowly. "You will obey every instruction that I give you. You will remain perfectly still otherwise. And you will remain silent unless I ask you a question. When I ask you a question, you will answer me honestly."

"Are you going to make me call you 'Master' too?" April asked. "Or is it Mistress?"

Vicki's face remained impassive. "You've already broken a rule."

"You didn't say that we'd started."

"We've started," Vicki said firmly. "Talk back to me again, and this ends."

April bit back a retort.

"Good, you're learning. Now close your eyes."

April hesitated.

"Is there a problem?" Vicki asked.

"Why do I have to close my eyes?"

"Because in the darkness, there's nowhere to hide."

April glanced over at the closet. Although it was shut, she had a clear picture in her mind of what it contained. It suddenly hit her how crazy this was. She was alone in an apartment with a stranger who had a closet full of what was essentially torture equipment. Vicki said she had no intention of using any of it but that didn't stop April's pulse from racing.

"Look," Vicki said, "If you're uncomfortable with any of this, we can stop."

"No," April said. "I don't want to stop."

"Then choose." Vicki took April's hand. "Choose to hand control over to me. If you want to do that, close your eyes and trust me. You can feel safe with me."

Safe. Although she hadn't realized it, that was what she'd been wanting to hear. She took in a breath and shut her eyes.

April's senses took a moment to adjust. Then she could hear the near silence of the room, and could feel the soft fibers of the rug between her toes. Vicki let go of her hand, but April could still feel the woman's presence beside her, and the electricity radiating between them.

Vicki circled behind April and hooked her arms around April's body, pulling her gently back against her chest. "Now, I'm going to ask you some questions," Vicki said. "Let's start with something easy. What's your name?"

"April Reid," she replied.

"Why did you come home with me tonight?"

"Why did you bring me home with you tonight?" April couldn't help herself.

Vicki's arms tightened around April's body. "Do I need to tell you the rules again? *I* ask the questions. *You* answer them." Vicki's voice was soft but firm. "Why did you come home with me tonight?"

"I don't know," April said. "I wanted to get laid."

"But why me?" Vicki asked. "I was watching you. There were plenty of other women who were interested in you. You didn't give them a second glance. Why me and not someone else?"

"You looked like you could show a girl a good time," April said.

Vicki let out a faint chuckle. "Flattery will get you nowhere. Try harder. *Why are you here?*"

"Because I want you to fuck me."

"Close," Vicki slid a hand down the center of April's stomach, stopping just below her bellybutton. "But we're not quite there yet. How about this? Why did you ask me to show you what I do?"

"Because... I was curious," April said.

"Once again, you're close but not quite there."

April let out an exasperated sigh. "I don't know."

"I do." Vicki pulled her in tighter. "I could tell from the moment I saw you what kind of woman you are. Strong. Fierce. Wild. You came home with me because you wanted someone who could handle you. Someone who can take you, and tame you, and tear away your tough exterior to get to what's beneath it. To get to that part of you that's just pure, unbridled lust."

One of Vicki's hands crept down to the inside of April's thigh, the other, up to her chest. She brushed her fingers over April's nipples. "And when you found out that I'm a Domme, you wanted more than to give in to lust," she said. "You wanted to give in to all those dark desires that you barely even knew you had. Does that sound right?"

April let out a breathy whimper. With Vicki pressed against her, and Vicki's hands all over her body, she was finding it difficult to think. But her whole body told her that the answer to Vicki's question was yes.

"Let's try this another way," Vicki said. "Tell me about the time you were handcuffed to the bed."

April thought back to that night. "It was years ago, with an old girlfriend."

As soon as April started talking, Vicki slid her hand up April's thigh and into her slit, gliding her fingers up and down with the lightest of touches.

A moan fell from April's lips. "We... we got these cheap handcuffs from a bachelorette party," April said. "Afterward, we were in bed together, and we wrestled a bit, and she pinned me down and cuffed me to the bedpost." Just recounting the night made April even hotter.

"Why did you wrestle her?" Vicki asked. "Why didn't you just let her handcuff you?"

"I don't know," April said.

"Yes, you do. Think about it."

Vicki circled April's swollen clit with a fingertip. April's breath hitched. Her legs would have given out if she didn't have Vicki there to hold her up.

"Because... I didn't want to give up so easily."

"What's so bad about giving in, allowing yourself to be vulnerable?" Vicki asked. "Why is that so hard?"

April tensed. This was a little too personal.

"You don't have to answer that. Why don't you tell me what you liked about being handcuffed to the bed?"

April searched her mind. "I liked having that power taken away from me. My free will taken away from me. I liked that it forced me to…" How could April explain what that night had been like for her?

"Succumb to your desires?" Vicki whispered.

"Yes." April was unable to keep the desperation from her voice. She had no idea how long it had been, but she'd been ready for Vicki the moment she walked through the door to her apartment. Her body craved release. Her body craved Vicki.

"And what did that feel like?" Vicki asked, her fingertips still strumming April's bud.

"It felt so liberating."

For a while, Vicki didn't speak. All April could hear was the faint sound of Vicki's breath in her ear.

"Keep your eyes closed." Vicki took April's hand and pulled her across the room. "The bed is behind you. Sit down on the edge and lay back."

April obeyed. Vicki guided her hand back down to the crease of April's thighs, skimming her fingers up April's wet folds. April quivered on the bed.

"Had enough?" Vicki asked. "Do you want to come?"

"Yes," April murmured.

"All you have to do is ask."

April groaned. She had forgotten about Vicki's vow. She sealed her lips shut, determined not to give in. But she already knew it was futile.

"I can see how worked up you are," Vicki said. "How every stroke of my fingers drives you closer and closer to the sweet release." Vicki stilled her hand. "But I'm not going to allow it until you say please."

April covered her mouth with her fist, biting back a moan. She couldn't take much more of this torment. She needed Vicki so badly that it hurt.

"All you have to do is say the word."

Vicki slid a finger down to April's entrance and dipped it inside her. A single finger, only shallow enough to tease, nothing more. April whimpered again, her body screaming for the release that Vicki was keeping just out of reach.

"Please." The word fell unbidden from April's lips.

"What was that?" Vicki asked. "I didn't quite hear you."

"Please." April didn't care anymore. She needed to come right now or she would lose her mind. "Please!"

"Now that wasn't so hard, was it?"

The next thing April knew, Vicki plunged her fingers inside her. Then Vicki was on top of her, kissing her furiously. April's whole body began to quake. With Vicki's thumb on her clit and two fingers inside her, the ache in April's core began to build and build...

April cried out as pleasure burst from deep within and spread through her. She trembled with the aftershocks, her head thrown back.

But even as her orgasm faded Vicki didn't stop. Removing her thumb from April's sensitive bud, she continued to pump her fingers in and out, pushing against that spot inside which drove her wild.

"Oh god!" Soon, another orgasm followed, even more

powerful than the last. April clutched at the bedsheets as wave after wave crashed through her.

Finally, Vicki withdrew and kissed April again, more gently this time. April let the soft bedsheets engulf her. She wanted nothing more than to lie there forever, sinking into Vicki's lips.

But eventually, she had to come back to reality. "That was... wow."

Vicki collapsed next to her. "It wasn't bad for me either."

"But I barely even touched you."

"You didn't need to. Your submission is its own reward." Vicki traced a meandering line down April's thigh with her fingers. "Don't get me wrong, I'm not one of those types who doesn't like to be touched. But not tonight."

"Some other night, then?" April blurted the words out before realizing what she was asking.

"Sure. As long as it's vanilla only."

It wasn't hard to figure out what Vicki meant by 'vanilla.'

"Why?" April asked. "I don't want vanilla. I want more."

Vicki groaned. "Don't say that. You have no idea how much I want to say yes."

"Why don't you?"

"Because I don't do bratty submissives."

"What does that mean?" April asked.

"It means I don't mess with submissives who like to push back and test my authority," Vicki said. "I like my subs obedient and eager to please me. You are neither of those things."

April sat up and looked down at Vicki. "Sounds to me like you're afraid of a challenge."

"You're proving my point with every word you say."

"Teach me, then," April said. "Teach me how to be your submissive."

"I'm not looking for someone who needs to be tamed," Vicki said.

"I don't need to be tamed. I can be good."

Vicki laughed. "I've only known you for a few hours and I know that's not true."

"Please?" April asked as sweetly as she could.

Vicki scrunched up her brow. "You're serious about this?"

"Yes, I am."

"It isn't all fun and games. There are rules. Conditions."

"I can handle it," April said.

Vicki folded her hands behind her head. "How about this? There's a club downtown that a friend of mine owns. It holds a ladies-only night every other Tuesday. I'll meet you there the Tuesday after next and give you a real taste of what it means to be my submissive."

"A real taste?" April glanced over at the closet full of toys. "What exactly does that involve?"

"You'll have to wait and see," Vicki said. "And you're going to have to prove to me that you can behave."

"Okay."

"I'll write down the address for you."

"Can't you just text it to me?" April asked.

"I could if I wanted to," Vicki replied.

"What, I don't even get your phone number? You expect me to go to some club and just wait for you to turn up?"

"If you want to play the game, you have to prove to me how much you want it."

So, Vicki wanted to keep her on a string? April was

starting to regret her promise to be good. If Vicki was going to toy with her, it was only fair that April could toy with her back.

But for now, she would play by Vicki's rules.

"Okay," April said. "Write down that address for me."

CHAPTER FOUR

When April arrived at the library on Monday morning, Lexi was already there with her head on her desk.

"Good morning, Lexi," April said.

"Not so loud," Lexi mumbled.

"Don't tell me you went out again last night?"

"I did. I'm too old for this. Getting drunk, spending the night in some other woman's bed."

"I've been too old for that for years," April said. "And I'm younger than you."

Lexi looked up at her. "Why are you so cheerful today?"

April shrugged. "Because I didn't spend my Sunday night getting drunk."

"No, that's not it." Lexi studied April's face. "No way. Did you get laid?"

April sat down at her desk. "Maybe."

"I knew it! Was that on Saturday night?"

April nodded.

"What happened?" Lexi asked. "I thought you left after I did."

"I was going to, but then I met someone."

"And?"

"And I went to her place," April said. "It was a really nice place."

"Come on, you've got to give me more than that," Lexi said.

"You know how it is. One thing led to another, and…" Just thinking about it made April burn inside. "It was really, really hot. And kind of kinky."

"Oh? Are we talking 'furry pink handcuffs' kinky, or 'chains and leather' kinky?"

April flushed. "I'm not going into detail." Besides, truth was, it was something different altogether. But she couldn't explain that to Lexi. "Anyway, I'm meeting her again next week."

"Oh? Like a date?"

"I don't think so," April replied. "It sounds like she just wants a repeat of the other night." And so did April.

"I thought hook-ups weren't your thing?" Lexi said.

"This is the exception."

"Good for you. Didn't I tell you that it'd be fun? You've forgotten all about Christie too, haven't you?"

"Fine, you were right." April had barely thought about Christie all weekend. And she hadn't been worrying about all the problems with the library as much as she should have been.

"I'm glad one of us got something out of Saturday night," Lexi grumbled.

"What happened with the woman you took home?"

"She was a total pillow princess. I made her come four times, but when it was her turn, she gave up after a few minutes. Who can come in three minutes?"

April had come in three minutes on Saturday night. Well, at least she had the second time. She hadn't even known that she was capable of orgasming more than once.

She felt so conflicted. She hated that Vicki was able to command her body like that. She hated even more that Vicki was able to get into her head, to turn her into a begging mess. April didn't beg. She didn't let others control her. Yet, Vicki had wrested control from her effortlessly. And April had enjoyed every moment of it. All those presumptions Vicki had made about what April really wanted? They were completely true.

April had tasted submission. She wanted more.

But next time, she wouldn't give in quite so easily. Next time, she'd make Vicki work for it. It was bad enough that Vicki had her on a leash, making April wait over a week to meet her at some club without so much as a phone number.

"Are you still thinking about the other night?" Lexi asked. "You're not falling for this woman, are you?"

"God, no," April said.

After she had left Vicki's apartment and the excitement of the night had faded, April had remembered what Vicki was really like. Cocky. A player. Vicki probably saw April as nothing more than another conquest. She could tell that Vicki's dominant personality wasn't limited to the bedroom. April had no interest in a relationship with someone as stubborn as herself. It would be a disaster.

"It's all just raw physical chemistry," April said. "We are completely incompatible otherwise."

"Well, be careful," Lexi said. "I know you haven't done the 'casual' thing before, but there's a risk of one of you developing feelings. It happens a lot, and it never ends well. Someone usually ends up getting their heart broken. Or worse, they end up falling in love and moving in together."

"You don't have to worry about that," April said. She switched on her computer. It was time to get to work.

"By the way, you might want to check your inbox," Lexi said. "The mayor's office sent out an email about the town hall meeting tonight."

The meeting had been called to give the community a chance to voice their concerns about the impact of all the new developments in West Heights. April was planning to attend on behalf of the library, but she had low expectations. The mayor and the city council supported all the new developments in West Heights because of the money that was coming in with them. The concerns of the existing residents were barely on their radar.

"Apparently, a representative from Oasis Developments is coming to speak to everyone," Lexi said. "It's probably some PR person whose job it is to convince the locals that bulldozing Oakmont Street to make room for luxury apartments is a good thing."

April found the email in question and skimmed through it, confirming what Lexi had said. "Maybe this is our chance to make Oasis listen to us about the library."

"I wouldn't hold my breath," Lexi muttered.

April ignored her. This could be April's last opportunity to save her library. Oakmont Street Library had been struggling for a while now. The library was unusual in that it relied more heavily on private funding than money from the city. The building itself had belonged to a wealthy philanthropist who leased it to the city for a token amount. But when the owner had passed away unexpectedly, his family had put his estate up for sale.

In the ensuing months, April had scrambled to save the library. Fundraising, soliciting donations, applying for state and federal grants. It wasn't enough. Property in West Heights was now at a premium. And so, Oasis Developments had snapped up the building.

Now, they had 90 days to leave the premises. Because the city didn't have the funds to buy or rent a space for the library in West Heights, they would be forced to close their doors. There were no options left.

Unless April could somehow convince Oasis Developments not to tear the building down.

"I'm going to that meeting," April said. "Whoever this representative is, I'm going to make them understand how important a role the library plays in the community. They can't just demolish it. They've already torn down half of West Heights. Corporations are taking over, people who have lived here for decades are being forced out because rent is too high. I may not be able to save the entire suburb, but I'm not going to give up on the library."

"Look, I'll come to the meeting tonight too," Lexi said. "But do you really think you can fight a corporation like Oasis?"

"I don't know, but you bet your ass I'm going to try."

"I know this place means a lot to you, but you have to be realistic. West Heights has already been changing for years."

What Lexi was saying was true. Fifty years ago, the historic suburb of West Heights had been mostly working-class families and immigrants. Fifteen years ago, the artists, musicians, and students started moving in. Everyone had quickly learned to coexist, creating a diverse melting pot. But with corporations like Oasis taking over, all of those people would be pushed out, and West Heights would never be the same.

"This is different," April said. "I'm not going to let West Heights be taken over."

"Well, no matter what happens, I'll be there to back you up," Lexi said.

April settled into her chair. She had to prepare for the meeting. Tonight, April was going to stand before this representative from Oasis Developments and present her case for why the library needed to remain open. She didn't know if it would make a difference. But one thing was certain.

She wasn't going down without a fight.

That evening, April left her apartment and headed to the town hall meeting. It was being held in the auditorium of the local high school. She gazed wistfully around at the neighborhood as she walked. This place that she'd called home for so long was changing right before her eyes.

A few people greeted April as they passed her on the street. April had worked at the library for years, so she knew everyone who came in. Most of the community went to the library for one reason or another. To borrow books, to use the computers, to meet up for activities and clubs.

West Heights needed the library. April wasn't going to let it get torn down.

When April reached the hall, the meeting had just begun. Mayor Collins was speaking on the stage, and a handful of council members were seated behind her. April was surprised that the Mayor had come in person. She was even more surprised that the hall was packed. She'd been to a few of these meetings before when there were matters relating to the library on the agenda, and the room was usually half empty.

It made sense. The library wasn't the only thing being displaced by Oasis. Not only had Oasis bought the library, but they had also bought all the surrounding apartments and houses. Even a small park, the only one for miles, was on the firing line. Most of the attendees appeared to be older people who had lived in the area their whole lives. They likely felt even more strongly about the changes taking place in their home than April did.

April scanned the seats looking for Lexi's black curls, which she always wore piled up on her head. Spotting her, April crept down to the aisle and took a seat next to her a couple of rows from the front.

"What did I miss?" she whispered.

"Not much," Lexi replied. "Collins is talking about new building regulations."

Mayor Collins was one of April's least favorite people. It was clear that she cared more about the more affluent parts of the city than West Heights. She was responsible for the funding cuts to the library over the past few years, and she supported all the new developments that were going up around the city, including on Oakmont Street.

Mayor Collins seemed to dislike April just as much as April disliked her. They had clashed a few times over the library, even before Oasis bought the building. April suspected Mayor Collins was glad that it was being shut down.

April tried to settle in and listen to the mayor, but she found herself getting restless. After a sleep-inducing explanation of the height limit changes for new buildings on King Street, Mayor Collins moved on to the final topic of the night.

"Now," she began. "The main reason I called this meeting was to give everyone a chance to discuss the effects of some of the upcoming development projects on the community. I've received a truckload of submissions about the proposed development on Oakmont Street, and I thought it could be helpful to have an open conversation about it. I invited Oasis Developments to join the discussion, and they've sent a representative to come speak with us." The mayor looked down at a sheet of paper in front of her. "She's the Vice President of Project Development. Hopefully, she will be able to address your concerns."

April frowned. With a title like that, this woman had to be high up in the chain of command. On one hand, it meant that she was someone who actually had the power to change things. On the other hand, she was probably some stuffy middle-aged woman in a suit who earned more in a day than April did in a month. She couldn't expect someone like that to be sympathetic to the residents of West Heights.

"Ms. Blake, was it?" Mayor Collins looked down toward someone sitting in the front row.

A tall woman with short blonde hair stood up and

walked toward the stage. Her back was to the crowd, her face hidden from view, but the upright, self-confident manner in which she held herself was very familiar to April.

Her stomach dropped. *No.* It couldn't be.

The woman climbed the stairs up to the stage and took her place next to the Mayor. "Please," she said. "Call me Vicki."

CHAPTER FIVE

This is not happening.

April simmered inside. There was no denying it. She had traded her jeans and blazer for a stylish, tailored pantsuit and heels, but otherwise, it was the same Vicki. Suddenly, the room felt too hot.

"Vicki it is," Mayor Collins said. "Vicki is in charge of the Oakmont Street project. She's going to tell us a little about the development, then we'll open the floor for questions. Vicki?" The mayor handed the microphone to Vicki and sat down on a chair behind her.

Vicki began to speak, but April didn't hear a single word. She was too busy trying to calm the emotions warring inside of her. Disbelief. Betrayal. Anger.

Desire.

Why, despite everything, did Vicki still provoke this reaction in her? In April's mind, it was clear—Vicki was the enemy. But her body said otherwise. Even though Vicki was more than twenty feet from where April sat, just being in the woman's presence stirred something deep within her.

Hearing Vicki's compelling voice brought back the memory of her lips on April's ear. Watching Vicki command the stage made April feel breathless.

Lexi nudged April in the ribs.

April blinked. "Huh?"

Lexi cocked her head at the stage where to where Vicki sat next to the Mayor. When had she finished speaking? Why was it that whenever Vicki was in the room, April would lose awareness of everything around her?

"Anyone?" Mayor Collins asked. "Based on the number of emails I get, I know you all have questions. Vicki is here to answer them. The floor is open."

The room remained silent. Clearly, no one wanted to be the first to go head to head with this corporate heavyweight. April didn't blame them. But she refused to be intimidated by Vicki.

She stood up.

"Ah, Miss Reid." Mayor Collins failed to keep her disappointment from showing in her voice.

Someone walked over to April and handed her a microphone. April's palms were sweaty. She usually didn't have a problem speaking in front of people. But her mind was awhirl with thoughts of Vicki.

She looked up at Vicki. If Vicki was surprised to see April standing there, she didn't show it. Maybe she didn't recognize April with the bright lights of the stage in her eyes.

Or maybe April was just a forgettable one-night stand to her.

"When you're ready, Miss Reid," Mayor Collins said.

Pulling herself together, April began. "I'm speaking on

behalf of the Oakmont Street Library, and all its staff and patrons." She had gone over these words in her head countless times, but she stumbled over them, her voice trembling. "It's been an important part of West Heights and the surrounding suburbs since the sixties. The library building is over one hundred years old. It's been a part of West Heights longer than any of us."

April took a deep breath and continued, her voice echoing through the hall. Slowly, she regained her focus. She had a job to do. She was not going to let her feelings about Vicki distract her from her goal. She was not going to let Oasis win.

She was not going to let Vicki win.

April finished her prepared points about the library, but she didn't stop. She was all fired up now. And she had so much to say. "This isn't just about the library. Other important, historic buildings and landmarks are being demolished all over West Heights. People's homes are in the firing line too. It's been happening the same way, over and over. Some rich developer will buy a block of apartments, then double, even triple the rent, sometimes illegally, until the tenants can't afford to pay anymore. They end up getting evicted, tossed out onto the street, unable to find anywhere to live because everywhere else in the area has had their rent raised too. Meanwhile, developers like Oasis will come in and bulldoze the buildings so they can build high rises, pocketing millions of dollars. They're destroying our beautiful suburb, our community, and the library is just a small part of that."

When April finished, her heart was pounding. She dropped her arms to her side, microphone in hand.

To her surprise, the entire audience started clapping.

Buoyed, April fixed her gaze on Vicki, her glare containing all her anger toward Oasis Developments, and all the other corporations taking over her suburb, and Vicki for being a part of it.

"Thank you, Miss. Reid," the mayor said. "Passionate as always." She turned to Vicki. "Vicki, is there anything you'd like to say?"

"Yes. Miss Reid, was it?" Vicki asked, a hint of amusement in her voice. "I agree, that was a very passionate speech."

There was no mistaking it—Vicki recognized her. She knew April was the woman she'd seduced and tormented. The woman who had been more than willing to yield to her command. And even now, Vicki's devilish smile—the very same one that had lured April to her that night at the bar—almost made April's legs give out from under her.

April stood up straighter.

"You should know that Oasis is taking all of this into consideration," Vicki said. "We're aware of the valuable services Oakmont Street Library provides, and we're arranging talks with the library's leaders to discuss how we can minimize the effects of the new development on the community."

"That's funny," April said. "Because I run the Oakmont Street Library, and I haven't heard a thing from Oasis since you bought the building."

Vicki tensed, a flicker of surprise crossing her face.

Not so smug now, are you? April thought.

But it didn't last. Vicki pulled at the front of her jacket, straightening it out. "You'll be receiving an email from my assistant first thing in the morning so that we can organize a meeting," she said. "I'd like to open up a discussion with all the staff at the library so we can figure out a suitable resolution."

"The only suitable resolution is one that doesn't involve destroying a hundred-year-old building and cutting people off from important resources that they need," April said.

"Let me assure you, Oasis is committed to minimizing the impact of this project on the community."

"You already used that line. How exactly are you going to do that?" April asked.

"That remains to be seen. It's why I'm going to work with you to make sure that the community is heard," Vicki said firmly.

"So we're going to sit down and have a chat, and then you're going to bulldoze the place anyway?"

"I will pass on your recommendations to the appropriate-"

"What, so that Oasis can just ignore them? Just like you people have been ignoring my attempts to contact you for months now?"

"You've made your point, Miss Reid," Mayor Collins said. "Why don't we hear from someone else now?"

April handed the microphone off and sat down. Vicki turned her attention to the rest of the audience. Although Vicki had lost her cool a moment ago, her infuriatingly self-assured demeanor had returned.

However, April had gotten everyone fired up. Hands were going up all around her. It seemed like everyone had something to say now. April's jaw almost dropped when Mrs. Evans, a quiet old lady who lived down the street from the library, launched a scathing tirade about how the Oakmont Street development project was pushing her friends out of the homes they'd lived in for decades.

April sat back and watched the proceedings with glee. To Vicki's credit, she handled it like a pro. But as the questions continued, she showed almost imperceptible signs of frustration. Vicki would cross her legs, then uncross them again a moment later, or would run her fingers through her hair a little too compulsively. Now and then, she would look in April's direction. And April would be staring right back at her, defiant.

After over an hour of this, Mayor Collins called an end to the meeting. It had already gone over time.

"If you have any further feedback, you can contact my office," she said. "We'll pass it along to Oasis. Thank you for coming, Ms. Blake."

"Please, it's Vicki," she said firmly. She turned, addressing the audience. "And please, feel free to contact me directly if you have any concerns."

April scoffed. She had no doubt that any emails sent Vicki's way would be palmed off to someone less important.

As everyone started to file out of the hall, Vicki and the mayor remained on stage, chatting with each other. Vicki glanced at April as she got up to leave, but April simply turned and marched toward the door.

"Whoa," Lexi said. "Wait up. Why are you in such a hurry?"

"I don't want to be in the same room with that woman any longer than I have to."

"Huh? You mean Vicki Blake?"

"Yes, her," April replied. "She's so... ugh! I can't stand her!"

"Well, you really showed her," Lexi said. "It was pretty awesome. We'll see if she follows through with her promise to work with us."

"I'm not holding my breath." April didn't trust Vicki as far as she could throw her, and she had no doubt that any meeting with Vicki would be fruitless. Right now, April never wanted to see or speak to Vicki ever again.

She would never work with Vicki Blake.

CHAPTER SIX

*A*pril refreshed her email inbox for the twentieth time that Tuesday. Here it was, almost time to go home, and nothing. "I knew I shouldn't have trusted that woman," she muttered.

Lexi looked across to April's desk. "Hmm?"

"Vicki! She said she was going to work with me. She said she'd be in touch. It's been a week now. I've called, I've emailed, I've left messages with her assistant, and nothing!"

"I'm not surprised," Lexi said. "I didn't know whether I should say anything or not because this isn't very professional, but I know a little about her."

April swiveled her chair to face Lexi. "What is it?"

"Well, in case you didn't already guess, she's a lesbian. So naturally, I've heard things." Ever the social butterfly, Lexi seemed to know every queer woman in the city. She always knew who was dating who, who was sleeping with who, and the latest in lesbian drama. "Vicki Blake has a reputation for being a player. And not in a good way."

April held back a curse. Her initial instincts about Vicki

were right. Although Lexi liked to gossip, she rarely spoke badly about anyone.

"She's either out causing trouble with some girl on her arm, or she's at Sapphire looking for someone to take home," Lexi said. "Not that there's anything wrong with that, obviously. But it's the way she goes about it. She charms women with her money and sweet words, then ditches them when she gets bored. It's like everywhere she goes, she leaves a trail of brokenhearted women in her wake."

April knew it. She never should have gone home with Vicki. That whole act Vicki pulled about not giving April her number was probably so that she could disappear without a trace. Today was the day that April was supposed to see her again. If none of this had happened and April went to that club tonight like Vicki had told her to, would the Vicki even show up?

It didn't matter. There was no way April was going to that club to meet Vicki. Not after all this.

Besides, even if Vicki had been telling the truth about seeing April again, she definitely would have changed her mind after the town hall meeting.

They were adversaries now, and Vicki knew it.

"I'm not surprised she works for a company like Oasis," Lexi said. "And I'm not surprised she hasn't kept her word."

"I can't believe her," April said. "Was she lying about wanting to work out a solution? Was she just trying to get me to lay off her at that meeting?" April's hands balled into fists on the desk. "If she doesn't get back to me soon, I'm going to go down to her office and confront her myself. She can't just make all these promises and then disappear!"

"Whoa, slow down," Lexi said. "Whenever you get all fired up, your first instinct is to go nuclear. That's not always the best idea."

"I'm just thinking about the library," April grumbled. "How else am I supposed to get her to listen to me? What else am I supposed to do?"

Lexi shrugged. "I don't know. That's why Eliza left you in charge, and not me."

Eliza. Lexi's words gave April an idea. She could pay Eliza a visit after work and ask for advice. Eliza had been the director of the library before April, and she had plenty of experience dealing with these kinds of issues. Eliza was both a mentor and a friend to April, and her cool demeanor meant that her perspective was always different from April's.

"I'd love to stay and help you work this out, but I have plans later," Lexi said.

"Let me guess," April said. "These plans involve a woman?"

"They might." Lexi gathered her things. "Hey, what happened with that woman you met at Sapphire? What was her name again?"

April's face grew warm. "I didn't say. It doesn't matter. I've decided not to see her again."

"Why not? Last week you were convinced she was some sort of sex goddess."

"I also said that we weren't remotely compatible. It's becoming more and more clear."

"That's too bad. Sorry it didn't work out." Lexi grabbed her coat from the back of her chair and headed for the door. "I'll see you tomorrow."

April remained at her desk, intending to get a little more work done. But her mind kept drifting back to Vicki. She opened up her web browser. Maybe she could find some other way to contact Vicki about the library. For the past few days, she had resisted the temptation to look Vicki up, to try to find out something about the woman who had been driving her crazy all week. But this was for the library after all. It had nothing to do with April satisfying her personal curiosity.

She typed "Victoria Blake" into a search, not expecting much. It was a common enough name. But to April's surprise, the whole first page of results appeared to be about Vicki.

That's odd. Abandoning her quest to find Vicki's contact information, April decided to dig. After all, it was important for her to know just who she was dealing with. She clicked through some articles about Vicki, most to do with her professional achievements. Several of them referred to her as the daughter of Harold Blake.

Naturally, that was a thread April had to follow. She searched for 'Harold Blake' and was met with even more results than she had gotten on Vicki. Harold Blake was the head of an international property development company that was worth billions and had been in his family for generations. Vicki's family.

That explained Vicki's fancy apartment, as well as Lexi's accusation that Vicki threw her money around to get women. Although April hadn't been seduced by Vicki's money, she was just another woman taken in by Vicki's charms.

It also explained Vicki's arrogance. With a family like

that, Vicki had probably lived a cushy, privileged life. No wonder she didn't give a damn about the people of West Heights.

As April stared at the screen, something caught her eye. The page on Vicki's father described Blake International as one of the biggest property development firms in the world. A company like Oasis had to be one of Blake International's competitors.

Why, then, was Vicki working for Oasis?

It didn't matter. Watching West Heights change over the past few years had proven to April that all those big multi-national development companies were the same. They wouldn't rest until every square inch of land, including national parks the world over, was covered with luxury high-rises, shopping malls, and office buildings.

April returned to her search for Vicki's contact information. All that came up was the same work email and phone number that April already had. Sighing, April sent off another email. She didn't know why she bothered. She would just get another canned response back saying that 'Ms. Blake would contact her as soon as possible.'

It aggravated her to have to chase Vicki for this. April hated the idea of begging Vicki for attention. But this was for the library.

And April would do whatever it took to save it.

———

After locking up the library, April made the short walk to Eliza's house. Too late, she remembered that Eliza had been away visiting her sister. April hoped she'd returned.

She reached Eliza's address. The small townhouse was one of the few remaining houses in the area that hadn't been bought out and torn down in preparation for new developments. The red brick facade was crumbling, and the door needed a new coat of paint, but April liked the familiarity of it. She'd grown up in one just like it. Of course, April's old family home had been replaced by a block of apartments several years ago.

April knocked on the door.

"I'll be right there," a voice called from inside. After almost a minute, a short, dark-haired woman with bright brown eyes opened the door. "April. Come in."

April followed her inside. The interior of the house matched the outside. The wallpaper was peeling off, and the floorboards creaked under April's feet.

Eliza walked slowly down the hall. She was barely forty, but the measured way she held herself made her seem decades older than she was. It was the result of a recently developed autoimmune condition that left her joints stiff. It was the reason Eliza had to quit her job as director of the library. April helped her out by picking things up for her from the store every now and then, but Eliza was too stubborn to accept anything more.

"Would you like something to drink?" Eliza asked. "I'm about to make tea." She was always drinking tea.

"Sure." April sat down at the kitchen table. "How was your trip?"

"It was great."

Eliza filled April in as she made tea in the kitchen. April wanted to help her, but she knew better than to ask. Still, it pained her to see someone she cared about struggling. Eliza had been there for April since the day they had met fourteen years ago. Eliza was a librarian at the time. She and a teen-aged April formed an unusual friendship, which April had sorely needed. Now that Eliza needed her, she wished she could repay the favor.

When Eliza was finished, she handed April a cup and sat down at the table across from her. "How did that town hall meeting go? I heard someone from Oasis came to talk to everyone."

"The meeting itself was great," April said. "Half the neighborhood showed up. But it didn't do much good in the end."

April recounted the events of the last week. Naturally, she left out the part about having sex with Vicki. Eliza listened calmly and silently, showing no reaction to April's growing frustration.

"It's been over a week now!" April said. "And I still haven't heard back from Vicki."

Eliza took a slow, thoughtful sip of her tea. "That woman sounds exactly like every other corporate big-shot I've had to work with," she said. "All evasive language and empty words. Unfortunately, these things always take time. A week is nothing. You've just got to keep on pressuring them."

"Keep pressuring them?" April said. "I don't have time for that! We have less than three months before they tear the place down, and I'm just supposed to keep sending them polite emails and phone calls?"

"April. You need to stop putting your heart before your head. That's not always a bad thing, but right now, you're letting your emotions control you. You look like you're ready to pick a fight."

April crossed her arms. Lexi had said something along those lines too.

"I understand more than anyone why you feel like you have to stand up for the library," Eliza said. "But sometimes, you have to slow down and think, and allow time for diplomacy to work."

"Okay. I'll be patient. But the moment I get Vicki on the line, I'm going to do everything I can to stop Oasis taking over."

"April," Eliza said. "You should be prepared for the fact that you might not be able to stop this."

"Why are you being so calm about this?" April asked. "You worked at the library for longer than I have. You've lived in West Heights longer than I have. The whole neighborhood is being taken over. It's not fair!"

"Life isn't always fair. And change is a part of life."

April huffed.

"You need to be more open to compromise. When the woman from Oasis finally gets back to you, don't just bully her into doing what you want." Eliza held up her hands defensively. "Sorry. Poor choice of words. What I mean is you should stay calm and talk with her civilly. Try to meet her halfway."

"Fine," April said. "I'll try."

"Look, since you're here, there's something I need to tell you," Eliza said. "When I was visiting my sister, she asked me to come and live with her." She placed her cup of tea down on the table. "I said yes."

"What? You're moving away?"

Eliza nodded.

"But you can't leave!" April said. "You've lived here your whole life. You love it here."

"I do. But as you know, my health isn't great. It would be good for me to have people around who can help me out a little. Plus, I can barely even get up these stairs anymore."

"But you have me here to help you," April said. "And all your other friends."

"I can't rely on all of you forever," Eliza said. "Also, my medical bills are starting to pile up. The developers who bought the place next door have been offering to buy my house for years now. I've always turned them down, but they recently made me an offer that's hard to refuse. April, it would mean that I'm set for life."

"But…" Tears began to form at the corners of April's eyes. She wasn't the type to cry at the drop of a hat. But she had known Eliza since she was fourteen. She had opened up April's world and introduced April to the sanctuary she needed so badly at the time. She had taught her how to stand up for herself and fight for what she believed in. She was April's guiding star.

And now she was moving away.

"You can always come visit me. It's only a short flight away." Eliza placed her hand on April's. "I'm sorry. I wish it didn't have to be this way."

"I understand." April blinked away her tears. "I should go. Thanks for the tea."

"Okay." Eliza gave her a sympathetic smile. "Try to remember what I said. Be open to compromise."

April nodded. As soon as Eliza let go of her hand, she fled out the door.

April stood on the sidewalk, wiping the tears from her eyes. She wasn't being fair to Eliza. But she was just so angry at the world right now. Everything was changing. Everything was out of her control. And there was nothing she could do about it.

But that didn't mean that she wasn't going to try.

She would take Eliza's advice about being open to compromise. But she wasn't going to sit around and wait for Vicki any longer. April needed to track her down, figure out a way to see her face to face. It wouldn't be easy, with Vicki ignoring April's attempts to get in touch.

There was one option. It was Tuesday night, and April knew exactly where Vicki was supposed to be.

It was a long shot. But April had to take it.

CHAPTER SEVEN

When April got home from Eliza's, she only had an hour before she was due to meet Vicki at that club. After a quick shower, she looked up the address that Vicki had given her, hoping to find out the name of the club. However, there was no information about it online at all. It was like it didn't even exist.

Was this some kind of joke? Had Vicki been messing with her all along? April sighed. It wasn't like she had any other options. She threw on a simple black dress that was somewhere between casual and dressy, and headed straight to the club before she lost her resolve.

April arrived at the address with a few minutes to spare. She double-checked the number next to the small, black door in front of her. *This is it.* Once again, she wondered if Vicki was messing with her.

April looked up at the sign above the door. It read *Lilith's Den* in red cursive script.

Lilith's Den? April had taken a class on mythology at

college, and although she had forgotten most of what she'd learned, she was pretty sure that Lilith was a demonic seductress from Jewish folklore.

And April was marching right into her den.

Two women walked around April to get to the door. They were both dressed in long black coats. One was wearing thigh-high leather stiletto boots with laces all the way up the front. The other wore a spiked leather choker around her neck that resembled a collar.

What the hell is this place? When Vicki mentioned a club, April assumed she meant a nightclub. What if this was a different kind of club entirely?

It didn't matter. April wasn't planning to stay. She would go in, find Vicki, and make her set a meeting there and then. That was it.

Steeling herself, she followed the couple through the door.

April was met with a small lobby, all painted black. A large, burly woman in a suit stood by a set of doors which led to the club inside. Another woman sat behind a small desk beside the door, a tablet in her hand.

The woman at the desk greeted the couple in front of April, waving them through. The bouncer opened the door and let them inside. April caught a glimpse of the flickering lights beyond before the bouncer pulled the door shut.

"Can I help you?" the woman at the desk asked.

"Someone invited me here," April said. "A friend."

"Are you on the list?"

Great, a list. Vicki hadn't said anything about a list. "I don't know."

The woman looked her up and down skeptically. "Name?"

"April Reid."

The woman tapped at the screen on her tablet, frowning.

April's shoulders sagged. It was unlikely that Vicki had bothered to put her on the list, especially after everything that had happened. Coming here was a stupid idea.

"There," the woman said. "April Reid. You were invited by Victoria Blake?"

"Yes," April stammered.

"Then she's responsible for you while you're in here. You'll need to sign these." The woman grabbed a clipboard from under the desk and handed it to April.

"What is all this?" April asked, flicking through the pages.

"Club rules, waivers, a non-disclosure agreement. The usual."

The usual? What had April gotten herself into?

"A first-timer, huh?" The woman asked.

April nodded.

She smiled. "I know how scary going to a BDSM club for the first time can be. Don't worry, you're in good hands with Vicki. She's one of our regulars."

A BDSM club. Of course Vicki would spring this on her. Was this supposed to be some kind of test? Was Vicki trying to scare her, to see whether April was serious about being her submissive? It didn't matter. April wasn't interested in that anymore. She did not want a repeat of the other night, no matter how much the thought of it turned her on.

Maybe this was a bad idea.

"Is everything okay?" the woman asked.

"Yes," April said. "It's fine."

She sighed. She was going to regret this. Without even reading the documents, she scribbled her signature at the bottom of each page and handed the clipboard back to the woman.

"Great." The woman gestured toward the door. "Welcome to Lilith's Den."

The bouncer opened the door wide. Focusing her mind on her goal, April strode into the club.

Music assaulted her ears. The dimly lit room was filled with women, drinking, talking, dancing. It almost looked like any other club. However, the patrons were mostly dressed in black, with only flashes of other colors to be seen. Some, like April, wore dresses. A few wore suits. Others wore lacy corsets or elaborate contraptions made of straps and leather. April's jaw dropped when a woman edged past her wearing nothing but latex pants and duct tape over each nipple in the shape of an X.

The club itself? It contained the usual tables and chairs, and there was a bar at one end. But around the room were all sorts of unusual pieces of furniture, some of which had people tied to them. A large wooden cross, a horse-shaped bench. Most of the crowd's attention was turned toward the large stage at the far end of the room where a woman was being led around on a leash.

April stood rooted on the spot, staring at everything. For the second time that night, she felt the urge to turn around and walk out the door.

Then, she spotted Vicki.

Wow. Vicki looked even hotter than she did the night

April had met her at the bar. She was sitting in the corner, lounging lazily on a chair, her legs crossed. She wore tight leather pants and a matching jacket, with a loose black top underneath and heeled leather boots. She wouldn't have looked out of place on the cover of a high-end fashion magazine.

Vicki sat alone, a martini glass in her hand. There was this empty zone of space around her as if no one dared to approach her. But more than one woman in the crowd was looking Vicki's way, eying her with either jealousy or adoration. Vicki didn't pay them any mind.

She tossed back the last of her drink, placed the glass on the table, and sat back, scanning the room idly. Almost immediately, Vicki's eyes fell on April.

Shit. There was no turning back now.

Summoning all her strength, April marched purposefully toward Vicki. As she approached, Vicki's lips curved up into a smile, one that seemed to say, *I knew you'd come.* But April hadn't come for Vicki. This was purely about the library.

"Hi April," Vicki said.

"Don't 'Hi April' me." April put her hands on her hips. "I've been trying to get hold of you all week!"

Vicki stretched her arm out over the back of the chair. "Miss me that much, did you?"

April scowled. "You said you'd contact me. About the library, I mean."

"I did say that. But I've been busy."

"Busy? So busy that you couldn't even send a single email?"

"I was out of town dealing with a work emergency. I wouldn't have been able to meet with you anyway."

"You could have told me that instead of leaving me in the dark," April said. "I guess the library isn't high enough on your list of priorities."

"Look." Vicki stood up to face April. "I didn't forget. I wasn't ignoring you. I've simply had my hands full all week."

"Are you sure that's why?" April asked. "It wasn't because you found out that the woman you slept with is the same one standing in the way of your development project and you didn't want to face me?"

"Although it was quite a surprise, I don't let business get in the way of pleasure," Vicki said.

April let out an exasperated sigh. "I don't have time for your games."

"I mean it. And I'm being honest. I was always going to meet with the head of the library. Public opposition to this project is high, so it's something Oasis needs to address. But I haven't had a spare moment for the past week."

"You weren't too busy to come here tonight," April said.

"That's because I told you I'd be here," Vicki replied. "I came here for you."

April felt a twinge of desire at Vicki's words. Her stupid, traitorous body. "You didn't seriously expect me to come here after everything that's happened?"

"You're here, aren't you? You came here for me too."

"Yes, but... No! I came here because you've been dodging my calls and emails. I decided I needed to find you and speak to you in person."

"I'm very glad you did, April." April's name seemed to roll off Vicki's tongue.

"Don't use your seductive bullshit on me," April said. "I saw through that smile of yours the moment we met. And I came here because I wanted to talk to you about the library. That's it."

"Really?" Vicki asked. "So this has nothing to do with the other night and how incredible it was?"

Heat rose through April's body. "No, it doesn't. I came here to try to see if we could work together to come up with a solution for the library. But it's clear that your mind is only on one thing."

"Can you blame me? You're not the only one who enjoyed the other night."

"Dammit, Vicki, can't you take this seriously?"

"Okay, fine." Vicki combed her fingers through her hair. "Here's the deal. This project is going ahead. There's nothing you can do to stop it. But I meant it when I said I will work with you to try to minimize the impact-"

"That's not enough!" April said. "We both know that's not going to be enough. If you're going to go ahead with this project, I'm going to do whatever it takes to stop you."

"You can try, but it's not going to change anything," Vicki said. "Be reasonable. Work with me here."

"I'll never work with you."

"Look, I get it. You're feeling betrayed because you found out I'm on the opposite side of this crusade you're on."

"I'm not on a crusade!" April glanced around. They were attracting more than a few stares. She lowered her voice. "And I don't feel betrayed. I never felt anything toward you to begin with."

"All right, you keep telling yourself that," Vicki said. "Whatever it is that you feel or don't feel toward me, don't let your emotions get in the way of us working together to do what's right for the library."

April cursed under her breath. As much as April hated to admit it, Vicki was right. Her anger toward Vicki was clouding her judgment. Maybe Lexi and Eliza had a point about April's tendency to act on her feelings without thinking.

"How about we meet next week?" Vicki asked. "I'll come by the library, and we can have a meeting with all the staff. Wednesday morning. It's the earliest I can do. How does that sound?"

April took a deep breath, attempting to settle the emotions roiling inside her. "All right. Next Wednesday morning."

"I'll have my assistant call you in the morning to confirm. I promise."

April nodded. Almost at once, a huge weight fell from her shoulders. But the turbulence within her remained.

April had been afraid of this. Afraid that it wasn't really the situation she was angry about. It was Vicki. And maybe it wasn't just anger that April was feeling toward her. Her eyes traveled down Vicki's body. April couldn't deny how incredibly sexy she looked in all that leather.

Vicki smiled. "Is that all you want from me? Because my offer still stands?"

"Your offer?" April asked.

"You know, the real reason you're here."

April scoffed. "I don't know what you mean."

"Yes, you do," Vicki said. "You want me to show you what a Domme can do."

April's said nothing.

"Or maybe I'm mistaken," Vicki said. "Maybe there's some other reason your cheeks are that lovely, rosy shade of pink. Some other reason you can barely meet my gaze. Some other reason you're still standing here with me."

"I…" April's tongue seemed stuck to the top of her mouth.

"Vicki?" A voice said from next to them. "I hope I'm not interrupting."

April turned to see a woman with pale skin and long, wavy black hair standing beside them. She, like April, was dressed in a simple black dress, but she somehow managed to look far more glamorous than April and anyone else in the room.

"Vanessa." There was a flicker of annoyance in Vicki's eyes. "I didn't know you were coming tonight."

"I thought I'd check up on the place," Vanessa said. "Make sure that no one is getting into trouble." She gave Vicki a pointed look.

"Trouble? Just because you've settled down doesn't mean the rest of us can't have any fun." Vicki seemed to remember April's presence. "April, this is Vanessa. Vanessa, this is April."

"A pleasure to meet you, April," Vanessa said. "So, this is who you begged me to put on the list, Vic?"

Begged? April got the impression that this woman was trying to embarrass Vicki. April looked from one woman to the other. She couldn't quite tell if this was friendly banter or veiled hostility.

Vicki ignored Vanessa's comment and addressed April.

"Vanessa owns Lilith's Den. She used to be the queen of this place too, until she got a girlfriend."

"I assure you, I'm still the queen of this place. And my girlfriend is right over there." Vanessa cocked her head toward the bar. "I'd be very careful what you say about her."

"I'm surprised you left her alone for a few seconds," Vicki said. "You two are usually joined at the hip. Aren't you scared someone's going to steal her?"

"You're the only person I've ever had to worry about trying to steal her. You know, she still hasn't forgiven you for stirring up trouble at that fundraiser. And neither have I."

"That was last year," Vicki said. "How many times do I have to apologize?"

"As many times as it takes," Vanessa replied.

April stifled a grin. It was satisfying to see Vicki thrown.

"I'd love to stay and chat, but we reserved a room upstairs," Vicki said. "Say hi to Mel for me."

"I'll pass along the message," Vanessa replied. "It was lovely to meet you, April."

"Likewise," April said.

Vicki's eyes followed Vanessa as she walked away.

"What was that about?" April asked.

"Vanessa?" Vicki replied. "Don't worry, that was just her being friendly."

"Friendly? I'm pretty sure she accused you of trying to steal her girlfriend." April remembered what Lexi had told her about Vicki's reputation for causing drama.

"I didn't try to steal her girlfriend. Vanessa can be possessive."

"Sure." April didn't believe Vicki one bit.

However, something about watching Vicki being dressed down by Vanessa had defused April's anger. And she couldn't help but wonder what kinky delights Vicki had in store for her.

April's curiosity got the better of her. "What did you mean about reserving a room?" she asked.

"I only said that to get rid of Vanessa," Vicki said. "I did reserve a room upstairs. But you've made it clear you're not here for that."

April hesitated. "What's upstairs?"

"Upstairs is where I teach you about being my submissive."

April's heart thumped. She had told herself that all she was going to do was talk to Vicki, then leave. She'd told herself that she wasn't going to do this. But as she looked into Vicki's jade eyes, she found herself wishing that Vicki would yank her in close and devour her with her lips like she had the night they met.

"So I wasn't mistaken," Vicki said. "You're still interested."

"I… might be," April said.

"It's simple." Vicki leaned in and spoke into April's ear. "Yes? Or no?"

With Vicki so close, April could feel the electricity sparking between their bodies. It would be so easy right now for April to just close her eyes and kiss her.

April exhaled slowly. She had gotten what she came for. She had gotten Vicki to listen to her. She had no reason to stick around. No reason not to walk out the door.

No reason not to give in to temptation.

"Yes," April whispered.

At once, Vicki's lips were on April's. The deep, overpowering kiss made April's world spin. *Vicki* made April's world spin. April knew this was dangerous, but she had no chance of resisting now.

Vicki broke away. "Let's go upstairs."

CHAPTER EIGHT

"So," Vicki said. "What do you think?"

April looked around the room. If the club downstairs looked like some sort of kinky dungeon, this room was much more imposing. It was painted a deep purple and was filled with more of the same strange furniture as downstairs, along with a bed. Arranged around the room on shelves and racks was a collection of BDSM toys that rivaled the contents of Vicki's closet.

April's stomach fluttered. The other night, when the two of them were recovering in Vicki's bed, Vicki had asked April which of the toys in the closet appealed to her. She hadn't known where to start. The restraints, those formidable looking whips—April wanted to try it all. As much as everything in this room intimidated her, it turned her on even more.

Vicki spoke again. "It's not too late to back out."

April turned to face her. "A minute ago, you were practically begging me to come up here with you. Are you sure you're not the one losing your nerve?"

"I mean it," Vicki said firmly. "If you're not comfortable with any of this, you can back out at any time. Or use your safeword."

"I know," April replied. "I wouldn't be here if I didn't want this."

"Remember," Vicki said. "A Domme's first priority is looking after her submissive. You're always safe when you're with me. I'll never push you further than you can handle."

April nodded. "Okay." She found Vicki's seriousness reassuring. "What are we going to do?"

Vicki smiled. "Since you were so interested in the toys in my apartment, we're going to play with some of them."

April folded her arms across her chest. "I thought you didn't need tools?"

"I don't. But they have their uses," Vicki said. "Especially when it comes to making unruly submissives more amenable."

Goosebumps sprouted on April's skin. What had she gotten herself into?

Vicki walked over to over to a padded leather table near the end of the bed. "Get onto the table on your hands and knees."

April looked at the sturdy black table. It was about waist height, and almost looked like a massage table, but it was clearly meant to be used for something more sinister. There were rings all around the edges that looked like something could be tied to them.

April glanced at the toys arranged around the room again. She and Vicki had briefly discussed what Vicki referred to as "limits" before they'd come inside. April knew that Vicki wouldn't cross any lines, but she wanted to know what the other woman had planned. "What are you going to do?"

"April," Vicki said. "What was my first rule?"

April thought back to that night in Vicki's apartment. "To obey your instructions."

"Get onto the table, before I make you crawl here."

April opened her mouth to retort, but Vicki gave her a frosty look that compelled her into action. "Fine." Without taking her eyes off the other woman, April walked purposefully to the table and climbed onto it on all fours.

Vicki took April's chin in her fingers. "What was my second rule?"

"To remain silent unless spoken to," April said.

"Do not break my rules again."

April nodded. The weight of Vicki's stare made her want to crumble.

Vicki brought her lips to April's in a knee-melting kiss. "Good," she said.

After the other night, April was starting to see a pattern in Vicki's behavior. Obey her, and Vicki would reward April with the kind of sweet, hot passion that made April weak. Disobey her, and Vicki would show April her much darker side. April couldn't help but wonder—what would Vicki do if April continued to defy her? How far could April push her?

Was she brave enough to try to find out?

"As for what I'm planning to do?" Vicki continued. "It's exactly what I told you the other night. I'm going to show you what it means to be my submissive. It's not all fun and games. And it's not all about sex, and pleasure. It's about power. It's about control. It's about you relinquishing both to me."

April knelt there in silence, her heart speeding up with every passing moment.

"You see," Vicki said. "You're the type of submissive that resists your nature. The type that fights your desires with every part of your being. You say you want this. In your mind, you want this. Your body gives it away too. And yet, you're still trying to hold onto control instead of letting go."

Vicki shrugged her jacket off her shoulders, placing it on a table to the side. She unclipped the watch around her wrist and placed it next to her jacket.

"So I'm going to start from the beginning," Vicki said. "I'm going to put you in the headspace of a submissive." She leaned down, her lips brushing April's ear. "I'm going to strip away all those layers of yours until all that's left is that primal part of you that craves this."

A frisson went through April's body. Vicki's words, her intense gaze, the raw, feminine power she exuded—it all should have frightened her. Maybe it did in a way. But it thrilled her even more.

April matched Vicki's fiery gaze with her own. "Go ahead and try."

A slight smile spread on Vicki's face. She walked over to a rack on the wall in front of April. It held a variety of whips, canes, and other tools, which could only be used for one thing. Vicki picked out a small leather paddle and returned to stand behind April, trailing her fingertips along April's back as she walked. April resisted the urge to turn and watch her, instead looking straight at the wall ahead.

But this left her staring at the rack of whips, which did little to settle the tempest within.

Vicki pushed April's dress up around her waist and caressed April's ass cheeks. She still had her panties on, but they were thin and cut high at the bottom, so they offered little protection. April's skin prickled.

"Remember when I told you that all of this is in the mind?" Vicki asked. "That's true even when it's physical."

April felt a stinging slap on her ass cheek. She sucked in a breath. It barely hurt, but it was a shock to her body and left her skin tingling. She screwed her eyes shut and waited.

"This isn't about punishment or pain," Vicki said. "It's about the experience of having control taken away. It's about the anticipation, the uncertainty, those seconds in between when you know what's coming, but you don't know when, or where, or what form it will take."

This time, Vicki rained down a series of short, sharp smacks on both her ass cheeks. April gasped, each impact rippling along the length of her body.

Vicki continued, punctuating every few words with a slap. "It's about how every strike sets you on edge and overwhelms your senses until you have no choice but to embrace your vulnerability."

April drew a breath in. She could feel the adrenaline pulsing through her, her nerves set alight. Every word Vicki said was right. April wanted this. Her body hungered for this. To throw away her inhibitions and let herself drown in everything she was feeling. With every stroke of the paddle, April felt all the walls inside her crumbling.

She closed her eyes and relaxed her body. She stopped resisting. She stopped fighting.

And it felt good.

A soft moan fell from April's mouth, spurring Vicki on. The other woman continued to rain blows down on April's ass, each stroke like a shock of cold water.

Finally, Vicki gave April one final slap on each cheek, then caressed them gently with the paddle. April purred. The smooth leather felt good on her burning skin.

Vicki rounded the table to stand in front of her. She cupped April's cheek. "Now, that wasn't so bad, was it?"

"No," April said softly, leaning into Vicki's hand.

"Maybe I was wrong about you. Maybe I can mold you into my perfect submissive after all."

Vicki drew April up to sit on the end of the table, then kissed her with surprising tenderness. April murmured with bliss. Her whole body was charged, and everywhere Vicki touched set off a spark. The kiss deepened, and Vicki's hands grew hungrier. Soon, there was a fire flaring inside April.

Vicki's slid a hand down to where April's thighs met and pressed her panties into her slit. "Do you want me to get rid of these?"

"Yes," April said breathlessly.

Vicki pushed April's shoulders down to the table and tugged her panties from her legs. She tossed them aside, then grabbed April's waist and pulled her to the very end of the table.

She parted April's knees and ran her fingers up the insides of April's legs. "A good submissive always gets rewarded," Vicki said.

April quivered, longing to feel Vicki inside her. Vicki

had other ideas. She grabbed hold of April's ass cheeks and dove her head between April's thighs.

April let out a gasp. Vicki's mouth felt divine. She sucked on April's nether lips, probed at her entrance with the tip of her tongue, circled April's swollen bud with a butterfly-light touch that drove April wild.

April grabbed onto the sides of the table with both hands. A part of her wanted to drop them to Vicki's head, to pull her in harder and guide her. The rest of her wanted to hand Vicki the reins, to give her body over to the other woman. So she closed her eyes and let Vicki take control.

And Vicki's control was absolute. This time, Vicki didn't try to draw it out. She didn't drive April to climax immediately either, even though she could have. Instead, Vicki ramped up April's pleasure steadily, until the fire inside her became a raging inferno.

"Oh god, Vic-" April jerked and writhed as tremors rocked her body. Vicki continued, her mouth unrelenting, her fingers digging into April's raw ass cheeks, until April fell back down to the table, limp and panting.

Vicki gave her a few moments to recover, then she leaned down and kissed April, stealing the breath from her lungs. She could taste her own arousal on Vicki's lips.

"Now you're going to do something for me," Vicki said.

Vicki guided April off the bench and drew her to the side of the bed. April's legs felt loose, and her ass ached, a satisfying, invigorating ache. Vicki stripped off April's dress and bra, then removed her own clothes piece by piece.

When Vicki was left in nothing but a pair of black panties, she pointed to them and issued April a command.

"Take these off for me," she said. "Without using your hands."

April blinked. How was she supposed to do that?

Oh. *Oh.*

Once again, the two parts of April—the part that wanted to resist, and the part that wanted to obey—were warring inside. She fixed her eyes on Vicki's. She would follow Vicki's instructions. But she wouldn't let Vicki know how much this was making her weak.

Slowly and deliberately, April got down on her knees. She leaned in and bit the waistband at the side of Vicki's panties, tugging them downward, then did the same on the other side. She worked them down Vicki's hips painstakingly, ignoring the fact that Vicki's pussy was right in front of her face. Finally, she had the panties past the swell of Vicki's hips, and she drew them down until they fell to the floor.

April stared up at Vicki, taking in her body in all its glory. It was the first time she'd seen Vicki completely naked, and she liked what she saw. Vicki's body was slender and toned, and she could see the faint outlines of her muscles underneath her skin. Her small nipples were barely a shade darker than her pale breasts, and at the apex of her thighs, her lips were covered in pale downy hair which glistened with moisture.

Vicki pushed her panties aside with her foot, then sat down at the very edge of the bed. "I'm going to let you show me how much you want to be my submissive. Show me how much you want me. Show me how much you want to please me," she said. "Once again, without using your hands."

This instruction was much easier for April to understand. She buried herself between Vicki's legs as Vicki had done to her minutes ago, the woman's heady scent enveloping her. She feathered her lips along Vicki's thigh, kissing the silky skin there, until she reached her prize. She slipped her tongue into Vicki's slit, savoring her taste. A satisfied groan emerged from Vicki's lips.

April smiled. Vicki might be the one calling the shots, but right now, April had the power to make her fall apart. And April was determined to exert this little sliver of control. She took her time, swirling her tongue over every inch of Vicki's pink folds before finally settling her lips on Vicki's clit.

Vicki shuddered, her face contorting in ecstasy. She threw her legs over April's shoulders and grabbed the back of April's head, pulling her in. Her rapturous cries only spurred April on. Soon, April felt Vicki's body tense.

"Fuck!" Vicki arched out, her hands leaving April's head to grip the edge of the bed. She bucked against April, her thighs hugging April's face.

Then she let out a breath and toppled backward onto the bed.

Afterward, April lay on her stomach in the bed, lost in a daze. Vicki had spent the last few minutes kissing April's raw, red ass cheeks, soothing them with her lips. Murmurs rose from April's chest. It felt heavenly. Was this part of what it meant to be Vicki's submissive? If it was, April could get used to this.

Vicki slid back up the bed to lie next to her. "How was that?" she asked.

"Good," April said.

"Just good? Is that all?"

"Fine, it was incredible."

"You know," Vicki said, "it would be easier for both of us if you would just obey me from the start."

April smiled. "Where's the fun in that?"

Vicki shook her head. "You're impossible."

"Someone has to keep you on your toes."

As the silence stretched out, April came back down to earth, and she began to remember why she had come to see Vicki in the first place. She had to make sure Vicki knew how serious she was about the library.

April propped herself up on her elbows. "So, about the library."

Vicki groaned. "Do we have to talk about that now? Can't it wait until the meeting?"

"We're here anyway so we might as discuss it. It's important to me."

"Okay. What do you want to discuss?"

"I want to talk about how we can keep the library open. The community needs the resources it provides-"

"Yes, I heard your little speech the other night. I'll do what I can, okay? I'll talk to the rest of the management team before the meeting and see what kind of solution we can work out. I don't know why I'm agreeing to this," she grumbled.

"Thank you," April said. Eliza had told her to compromise? This was her compromising.

"It's time to add a new rule," Vicki said.

"A new rule? Does this mean that you want to keep doing this?"

"Don't you?"

April thought for a moment. She should have zero interest in pursuing anything with Vicki. Even before everything with the library, she had her misgivings. But that didn't change the way April felt toward Vicki. That didn't change the fact that April was so inexorably drawn to her and the release that she offered.

Besides, Vicki seemed to be coming around on the issue of the library. So maybe they were on the same side after all.

"Yes," April finally said. "I still want to do this."

"Here's my next rule," Vicki said. "When we're together, no talking about work, or the library, or the development project. No discussion of it, no thinking about it. We leave all that at the door. Pretend that it doesn't even exist."

"Will you be doing that too?" April asked.

"I have no problems leaving business at the door. You're the one who came to me tonight, guns blazing."

"Fine," April said. "No work when we're together."

April could do that. And honestly, it might make things easier. She could just pretend that the Vicki she was pursuing this twisted affair with was a different person from the Vicki who she would have to negotiate the library's fate with.

"Good," Vicki said. "My old rules still stand. I expect your complete obedience when we're doing this. No talking back, no trying to push me. Nothing less than absolute submission. Can you do that?"

April hesitated. Everything Vicki was offering seemed contrary to April's nature. Maybe that was why she wanted it so badly. No matter the reason, there was no denying it—April was hooked.

"Okay," April said. "I can do that."

She would play this game with Vicki. Because that was all it was—a game. It wasn't true submission. April hadn't truly surrendered to Vicki.

And she never would.

CHAPTER NINE

The week that followed seemed to crawl by. April was so busy at work that she barely had a moment to herself. It didn't help that she spent half her time daydreaming about the night at Lilith's Den with Vicki.

It left her feeling so conflicted. She'd enthusiastically agreed to be Vicki's submissive. She loved the way submission made her feel.

But she hated that it was Vicki making her feel this way. Despite their agreement to work together on the library, April felt like their alliance was tenuous at best. She was still wary of Vicki, and she still found the blonde-haired woman irritatingly cocky. No amount of physical attraction, no matter how intense, could overcome that.

Despite it all, April played along with Vicki's games. And Vicki took her games very seriously. That night, they had discussed the finer details of their arrangement. Limits. Expectations. Even more rules.

One of Vicki's rules was that April had to send her a sexy photo every day. The photos were, in Vicki's words, a daily reminder of their agreement. This was one rule April was happy to follow. Whether it was intentional or not, Vicki hadn't been specific about what counted as 'sexy.' So April decided to be creative. She sent photos of herself to Vicki that were sexy but not revealing, enticing while still leaving a lot to the imagination. If Vicki wanted anything more than that, she would have to wait until they saw each other again.

A few times, Vicki had taken the bait, replying with a salacious message that made April blush. Other times, April's photos had been met with silence, and the only reason April knew that Vicki had seen the photo was because her phone showed the message as read.

April was determined not to let Vicki get inside her head. Nevertheless, she found herself thinking about Vicki constantly. That soft, golden hair that she was always playing with. Those piercing eyes. That enticing smile. Every time April closed her eyes, she was back in that room at Lilith's Den with Vicki, the scene playing out, over and over.

Of course, it wasn't Vicki herself that April was addicted to. It was the erotic game the two of them were playing together.

"April?" Lexi asked.

"Hmm?" April looked up to see Lexi squaring away her desk.

"The meeting? Vicki will be here any minute."

"Right." As Vicki promised, her assistant had called April a week ago to confirm the time and date.

"Hopefully it won't be a complete waste of time," Lexi said.

"It won't be. Vicki promised me she would try to work something out."

"She promised you?" Lexi asked. "I thought you said you talked to her assistant?"

"Yeah, I did. I spoke to Vicki herself too," April said, leaving out the fact that she had spoken to Vicki at a BDSM club.

"How did that conversation go? Did you yell at her some more?"

April crossed her arms. "Why does everyone think I'm some kind of tyrant?"

"Who else said that?"

"Eliza."

Lexi chuckled. "That woman is never wrong."

"I did yell at Vicki a little," April admitted. "But then she genuinely seemed to be interested in finding a solution. Maybe we have her all wrong."

"Seriously? A week ago, you were convinced that she was pure evil. What did she say to you that changed your mind?"

"Nothing. I'm just trying something new. I'm being open to compromise and change."

"Eliza?" Lexi asked.

"That obvious, huh?" April got up from her desk. "Let's go."

They made their way to one of the meeting rooms at the other side of the library. Vicki hadn't arrived yet, but everyone else had. As well as the library staff, a few community leaders who were involved in programs that took place at the library had been invited.

April greeted everyone, then sat down at the head of the

table, with Lexi to her right. She looked out through the glass walls of the meeting room, watching for Vicki's arrival. Moments later, Vicki appeared, dressed as stylish as ever in a pantsuit and heels. She looked so different than the last time April had seen her, all dressed in leather. But somehow, Vicki managed to look incredibly sexy no matter what she wore.

Vicki spotted them through the glass and strode purposefully toward the meeting room. The head librarian was a few steps behind, struggling to keep up with the long-legged woman.

The two of them entered the room. Vicki apologized for her lateness, then made her way around the table, introducing herself to the staff one by one. When Vicki reached Lexi, the curly-haired woman gave Vicki a stiff, firm handshake. Vicki returned it in kind.

What was that about? Perhaps neither of them liked not being the only lady-killing lesbian in the room. April made a mental note to ask Lexi about it later.

But April forgot all about it when Vicki moved on to her. April stood up and took Vicki's outstretched hand. As soon as their skin touched, April was transported back to the other night. Suddenly, the room felt foggy. Could everyone see how weak-kneed Vicki made her?

As soon as Vicki let go of her hand, April sat down before her legs could collapse underneath her.

Finally, Vicki took a seat at the opposite end of the table, right across from April, and placed a folder down in front of her.

"Shall we get started, April?" Vicki looked at April expectantly. "Sorry, do you prefer Miss Reid?"

It took April a moment to find her voice. "April is fine."

"April it is."

"Uh, yes." April wasn't sure if she imagined the suggestion in Vicki's eyes, but she ignored it. "Let's get started. Vicki, can you tell us about how Oasis is willing to work with us?"

Vicki flipped open her folder. "You'll be pleased to hear that Oasis has agreed to lease a property to the library at the same rate the city was paying for this building."

April frowned. Was it really that easy?

"We've recently acquired a property in Springdale which we've determined is an ideal location for the library."

"Springdale?" April said. It was a couple of suburbs away from West Heights. "Isn't that a bit out of the way?"

"It's not Oakmont Street. But with property in West Heights at a premium, there aren't any alternatives in West Heights itself. I assure you, the site is more than suitable. It's on Earlwood Street."

April knew the area. Not only was it nowhere near central West Heights, it was in one of the most crime-ridden parts of the whole city. Most people would never go there alone. And the library's most vulnerable patrons—the elderly, children—wouldn't dare venture there at all. Even if they wanted to, it was miles from the subway and bus stops. Most people in West Heights didn't own cars.

Not only that, but the funding that the library received from the city was dependent on how many customers used the library. If people stopped coming to the library, it wouldn't receive enough funding to stay open. The library would be as good as dead.

"So," Vicki said. "What are your thoughts?" Vicki looked pointedly at April.

The eyes of everyone at the table followed. They were looking to April for guidance. But her disappointment weighed so heavy on her that she found she couldn't speak. Vicki had promised to come up with a solution. This wasn't a solution.

Lexi swooped in to save her. "It's something," she said. "Do you have any more information about the site?"

Vicki flicked through the folder before her and pulled out some glossy printouts. "I've prepared some material for you to take a look at. Here." Vicki passed them around. "As you'll see, the site isn't as big as this one, but Oasis is willing to help out with some improvements."

April took a printout and flipped through it, trying to maintain her composure. But as she looked at the photo of the tiny, ramshackle building, her disappointment turned to anger. April didn't know much about real estate, but she was certain a property like this in such an undesirable location was useless to Oasis. It was no wonder they were offering to lease it to the city.

Vicki spent the next ten minutes explaining Oasis' offer in detail. After a while, the others began to ask questions. Were they actually on board with this?

"April," Vicki said. "I haven't heard from you yet. Do you have anything to add?"

"No," April said flatly.

"Then we're done here. If you have any questions, don't hesitate to contact me." Vicki's eyes landed on April's. "I'm committed to working with you on this."

April kept her eyes locked with Vicki's but said nothing.

Vicki stood up and straightened her jacket. "If you'll excuse me, I have another meeting-"

"Wait," April said.

"Yes?"

"Before you leave, I'd like to speak with you."

CHAPTER TEN

*O*nce the room had cleared, Vicki walked over to April's end of the table. "So? What do you think?"

"What do I think?" April stood up and dropped the printout onto the table before Vicki. "What is this, Vicki? You said you'd work with us!"

"I am. I don't understand what the problem is."

"The problem is that your solution isn't a solution at all. Do you really think the library can operate in some rundown shack in Springdale? We might as well just shut our doors now."

Vicki pulled out a chair and sat down. "I don't know what you were expecting. Oasis is being very generous. We don't normally do things like this."

"What, so we should be grateful for your charity?" April asked.

"*My* charity?" Vicki asked. "Is it Oasis that you're angry at? Or me?"

April threw her hands up. "You're leading the project,

aren't you? You're the Vice President of the company. As far as I'm concerned, this is all you."

"I'm VP of Project Development. I can only control what happens in my department. I still answer to the CEO and the board. I couldn't change what's going to happen to the library even if I wanted to. The gears are already in motion. The library's fate was sealed when Oasis bought the building."

"Then why did you tell me you'd see what you could do?" April asked, her voice rising. The room was sound-proof, but the walls were glass. Anyone could walk by and see the two of them arguing, but professionalism was the last thing on April's mind. "Why did you tell me you would work with me?"

Vicki stood up, her eyes darkening. "I *am* working with you. Why do you think I came to this meeting personally instead of sending someone else? I don't usually spend my workday traveling halfway across the city to meet with a bunch of librarians."

"A bunch of librarians?" April fumed. "So we're not worth your time? *I'm* not worth your time?"

"That's not- Will you just listen to me? I did what I could. I stuck my neck out for you. If it wasn't for me, Oasis wouldn't have even considered helping out the library. I've worked my ass off on this project. If it goes smoothly, I'm looking at an executive level promotion. And I'm risking it all because of you."

April scoffed. "I'm sorry that I'm standing in the way of you getting a bigger paycheck."

"It's not about a paycheck," Vicki said through gritted

teeth. "My job is more than just a job to me. But it's clear there's no point trying to make you understand."

"I'm not the one lacking empathy in this situation. You're the one who's rolling into a neighborhood that's hundreds of years old, displacing its residents and turning it into yet another exclusive playground for the wealthy. But I wouldn't expect someone like you to understand."

Vicki's eyes narrowed to slits. "Someone like me?"

"That's right," April said. "I know all about you, Victoria *Blake*."

Vicki recoiled. Had April hit a nerve?

But a moment later, Vicki regained her composure. "You've obviously made up your mind about me." Vicki picked up her folder. "I'm done trying to reason with you."

April shook her head. "I can't believe I actually thought this meeting would make a difference."

"You really don't get it, do you? This project is happening. In a few months, this building is going to be torn down. You're naive if you think there's anything you can do about it."

April put her hands on her hips. "Don't think I'm going to roll over that easily. I'm going to keep fighting for the library until it's a pile of rubble. And I'm going to keep fighting *you*."

"You can try," Vicki said. "But you're wasting your time."

"Just go," April said. "Get out of my library."

Vicki tucked her chair under the table. "If you come to your senses and decide you want to work with me instead of fighting me, let me know."

"That's not going to happen."

"Suit yourself." Vicki turned and headed for the door.

Before she left the room, she gave April a charming smile. "It was lovely to see you again."

April closed her eyes and slipped deeper into the bath, letting her head sink under the water. She liked how quiet and peaceful it was, submerged like this, how removed it made her feel from all her problems. The events of the day had left her feeling drained.

Most of all, she was feeling torn about Vicki. On one hand, she was angry. Did Vicki really think Oasis' offer would placate her? Was Vicki so out of touch, so used to everyone deferring to her, that she thought April would roll over without a fight?

But at the same time, April wondered if Vicki was being honest when she said that she didn't have any control over the fate of the library. Maybe Vicki was just like everyone else, answerable to someone above her. Maybe April was being too hard on her.

April watched the bubbles of her breath float to the surface. Why the hell was she trying so hard to find a reason to justify Vicki's actions? Why did April even care about Vicki's motivations?

She emerged from the water and took a breath. The relaxing music playing on her phone filled her ears and the scent of the rose petal bath bomb hung in the air. But it did nothing to calm her.

Giving up, April decided to try a distraction instead. Maybe a podcast would help take her mind off everything.

April reached up to the counter and picked up her phone. She had a message.

It was from Vicki.

Before April could stop herself, she opened the message.

I haven't received my photo yet today. You have two hours. The clock is ticking.

Every muscle in April's body tensed. Did Vicki really think April was going to send her a photo after everything that had happened today? She was delusional.

April couldn't help but feel like Vicki was taunting her. Vicki had never sent her a reminder like this, although, admittedly, it was getting late. The day was almost over, and time really was running out.

It didn't matter. April wasn't going to play Vicki's game anymore. And she didn't want to think about Vicki for one more second. From now on, her mind was a Vicki-free zone.

An hour and a podcast later, April slipped out of the tub and dried herself off. It was eleven p.m., so she threw on an old shirt, and got into bed.

April closed her eyes. A minute passed, then two, then five. She rolled over, trying to get comfortable, and caught a glimpse of her alarm clock. 11:15 p.m. She rearranged her pillows and rolled over again. Her mattress felt lumpy, and she kept getting tangled in her sheets. She looked at the clock. It was 11:23 p.m.

April let out a curse. She had been tired the whole day, but now, she was wide awake. There was no point lying in bed staring at the ceiling. Instead, she did what she always did when she couldn't sleep.

She opened up her drawer and pulled out a small, pink vibrator.

Underneath her covers, April slipped out of her panties and turned the vibrator on, settling it at the peak of her slit. She closed her eyes, letting the vibrations ripple through her. April had never really considered this something sexual. It was more of a way to blow off steam and release tension.

But tonight, it wasn't working.

She let out a growl of frustration and turned the vibe up a notch. Her mind began to drift back to the events of the day. Inevitably, her thoughts returned to Vicki. To that smug smile. That conceited way she held herself. That expectation that everyone bow to her. April had done just that, twice now.

And she had loved every moment of it.

A moan rumbled in April's chest. She slid her free hand between her legs, gliding her fingers down her folds. She thought about how good Vicki had made her feel that night at the club, how much every kiss of that leather paddle had made her body come alive, how quickly she had yielded under Vicki's dominating gaze.

April's body began to sizzle. She hated the way Vicki made her feel. Like she was drowning, like she was losing control—losing herself—in Vicki.

April slid her fingers inside her entrance, her mind swirling with fragments of Vicki. Vicki's fingertips grazing her skin. Vicki's lips, smothering the flame between her thighs. Vicki's essence, overloading her senses. Vicki's thighs quaking around her head. April didn't want to think about her right now. But she couldn't stop. And she was so close.

April turned up the little pink toy, giving herself one hard burst of vibrations. Her body overcome, she rose up, Vicki's name on her lips as she came.

She sank back into the bed, breathing hard. Whether April liked it or not, Vicki had wormed her way into April's head and wasn't showing any sign of leaving.

A quick trip to the bathroom later, and April was back in bed, her toy stashed away in her drawer. Without thinking, she glanced at the time. 11:54 p.m. Panic washed through her. She had vowed to stop playing Vicki's game. But April couldn't stop glancing at her phone. And with every passing second, her anxiety grew.

Sighing, April grabbed her phone. She thought for a moment. If she was going to do this, she could at least give Vicki something to think about. April pulled her vibrator out of her drawer, pointed her phone at it and snapped a picture. She sent it off to Vicki with only a minute to spare. Vicki could think whatever she liked about that.

Immediately, her phone buzzed.

Next time don't make me wait, Vicki's text said.

As April stared at the message, something dawned on her.

Vicki had been waiting for April's photo.

Vicki was annoyed that she had to wait.

Vicki wanted April just as much as April wanted Vicki.

Vicki needed April's submission just as much as April needed to submit.

April smiled. Vicki might have the upper hand now, but the game wasn't over yet.

CHAPTER ELEVEN

*A*pril sat in the lobby of Oasis Developments, waiting for Vicki.

After the other night, when April had caved and sent Vicki the photo, their affair continued as it had before. April knew it didn't make sense. Vicki was the last person she should have been doing this with. But she couldn't deny how intoxicating she found Vicki, and how much playing Vicki's game excited her.

It was almost like there were two Vickis. One of them was the stuck-up corporate businesswoman who was determined to bulldoze April's beloved library and filled her with righteous fury. The other was the seductive siren who filled April's every waking moment with dreams of submission.

So April told herself that the woman she'd spent those nights with was a different person than the Vicki she'd fought with in the meeting room that day. After all, wasn't April a different person when she was alone with Vicki? The defiant submissive she pretended to be was different than the person April was day to day. In April's mind, the two worlds they existed in were completely separate.

So, April continued to follow Vicki's rules. But that didn't stop her from mounting her own little rebellion. Every day, she would send Vicki a photo just before midnight. At first, it was because she felt conflicted about her attraction toward the woman. After a few days, it became deliberate. April imagined Vicki sitting at home every night, staring at her phone and waiting for April's photo to come. When it did, April made sure the photo was something provocative.

April relished this little slice of power she had over Vicki. She had the ability to get under Vicki's skin. She had the ability to drive Vicki wild. She still had some control. They were on equal footing after all.

With this in mind, April decided to try to talk to Vicki about the library once more. After she'd had a few days to cool off, she had realized that she hadn't actually explained to Vicki the reason why Oasis Developments' proposed solution wasn't enough. Once again, she'd let her temper run away with her. April wasn't usually quite this hot-headed. Vicki had that effect on her.

April messaged Vicki's personal number to set up a meeting. She felt like she was breaking some unwritten rule, mixing business with pleasure, but Vicki didn't comment on it. She agreed to squeeze April in for a short meeting, but due to her busy schedule, April would have to come to her.

Which was how April found herself in the lobby of Oasis Developments late one afternoon.

She shifted in her seat, glancing idly around the lobby. The lavish office was a glaring reminder that Vicki lived in a completely different world from April, one where even the receptionist wore designer clothes and looked like a model. Could she ever expect Vicki to understand her point of view when it came to the library and West Heights? April suddenly felt like she was deep in enemy territory.

A woman, presumably Vicki's secretary, came out into the lobby and led April to Vicki's spacious office. When April entered the room, Vicki was sitting in a chair behind her desk, having a heated conversation with someone on the phone.

"That application should have been submitted three months ago," she said. "Someone in your department dropped the ball. You need to fix this." Vicki paused, no doubt listening to some poor pencil-pusher's excuses. "I don't care. If you want to keep your job, you have three days to sort this mess out."

Vicki looked up at April, nodding at her in greeting. She gestured for April to sit down at a small glass coffee table by the window.

April took a seat. There was a strange desk toy on the table before her, a small contraption consisting of tiny chrome balls and moving arms on a wooden base. It seemed out of place in Vicki's modern, minimalistic office. April pushed one of the balls, causing the entire thing to rotate and swing. She watched its hypnotizing movements while she waited.

After a few more minutes, Vicki finished with her phone call.

"April. Thanks for coming," she said.

"No problem," April replied.

The room fell silent. Both of them had cooled off since

their heated encounter in April's office. But there was a hint of tension in the air.

"Would you like a drink?" Vicki walked over to a cabinet in the corner behind April and opened the door, revealing a small fridge and an assortment of liquor.

"You have a mini bar in your office?" April asked.

"I'm here a lot. Sometimes I feel like a drink after spending twelve hours at work."

It shouldn't have surprised April that Vicki worked so much. It was clear from her job title that she was high up in the ranks. But Vicki always seemed like she coasted through life effortlessly. The idea of Vicki slaving away behind a desk seemed to clash with April's impression of her.

Of course, the desk Vicki slaved away behind looked like it cost a fortune.

"So, would you like a drink?" Vicki asked.

"Sure," April replied. "Whatever you're having."

Vicki produced two glasses and a cocktail shaker and set about mixing a simple drink. She divided it between the two glasses, and brought them over to the table, handing one to April. April took a sip. It was rum mixed with something. She wondered if Vicki chose the drink because she remembered that April was drinking mojitos the night they met.

Vicki sat down across from April, her lean body stretched out in the chair. The sun was still out, and the sunlight streaming through the window made her hair look like spun gold and made her green eyes sparkle.

"Was there something you wanted to talk about?" Vicki asked. "Or did you just miss me?"

April ignored Vicki's quip. "I've been thinking about

other options for the Oakmont Street Library. I'd like to discuss them with you."

"Eager to get down to business, are you?"

"You said we only had half an hour."

"My evening meeting was canceled. We have all the time in the world now." Vicki sat back and crossed her legs. "Why don't we take a step back? Tell me about your history with the library."

"Well, what do you want to know?" April asked.

"How long have you been working there?"

"Almost ten years all up. I worked there in high school as a page, but I stopped when I left for college. I ended up working there again after I came back to West Heights."

"Do you enjoy your job?" Vicki asked.

"Yes," April replied. "It's not like I dreamed of working at a library my whole life, but I was offered a job there after college and I haven't looked back."

Vicki took a sip of her drink, studying April over her glass. "Why is saving the library so important to you? The way you talk about it makes it seem like it's about more than just your job."

"You're right," April said. "The library is special to me. I have my reasons for wanting to save it."

Vicki waited for April to elaborate. But April was reluctant to share something that personal with her.

Vicki's words reminded April of something she had said last time they spoke. "You told me that your job was more than just a job for you too. That your promotion wasn't about a paycheck. What did you mean by that?"

Vicki crossed her legs. "It's a chance to prove myself."

"To who?"

"It's personal."

Considering her own reticence, April couldn't fault Vicki for being tight-lipped. Everything between them felt so tenuous, like a truce that could devolve into conflict at any moment.

As April placed her drink down on the table, her eyes fell to the chrome trinket in front of her. Somehow, it was still spinning. "What is this?"

"I have no idea," Vicki said. "My father gave it to me."

"Your father is the Head of Blake International, right?"

"The one and only." There was a touch of irritation in her voice.

April pressed on. "Isn't Oasis one of their competitors?"

"It's Blake International's biggest competitor in the country," Vicki said. "I didn't know you knew so much about the world of property development."

"I don't," April said. "When I heard that you were leading the Oakmont Street project, I decided to do some research. Your family came up when I searched your name online."

"Of course they did." Vicki sighed almost imperceptibly. "There's no escaping the Blake family name."

"Why would you want to?"

Vicki didn't answer her. Not at first. "All of this," Vicki said, gesturing around the room. "My job, my life. You think my success is because of my family, don't you?"

"Well, I…" April hadn't forgotten how she'd thrown Vicki's family name at her that day they had argued in April's office. Or how Vicki had reacted.

"I'm not successful because of my family." Vicki stilled the spinning chrome ball contraption with her hand. "I'm successful in spite of them."

Silence hung in the air. April sipped her drink. It was strange, that they knew so little about each other, yet they had been so intimate, had shared parts of themselves that others never got to see.

"You know," Vicki said, drumming her fingers on the arm of her chair. "You've been cutting it close with your photos lately."

April flushed. "I thought we were keeping business and pleasure separate."

"Actually, I said that we won't let business get in the way of pleasure, not the other way around."

"I don't see what the problem is," April said. "I've sent you a photo every single day like you asked. I haven't broken any of your rules."

"One of my rules was 'do not test me.'"

"Maybe you should have made your rules more specific."

Vicki leaned across the coffee table, speaking in a low voice. "You're very lucky there's an office full of people outside those doors, otherwise I'd do something about your attitude."

April bit back a smile. "What exactly would you do?"

"I'd bend you over my desk and spank you."

Desire flared inside April's body. Vicki's commanding gaze had April mesmerized. At that moment, April knew that if Vicki ordered her to bend over her desk right now, she would be powerless to refuse.

No, she wouldn't even want to refuse.

Vicki straightened up and brushed her fingers through her hair. "But, like I said, there's an office full of people out there. And we have business to attend to."

April blinked. *Right.* She pulled herself together. How

was it that after all this time she was still susceptible to Vicki's charms?

"You want to discuss options for the library?"

"Yes." April recalled Eliza's advice. *Be civil. Be open to compromise.* "The problem is, the solution Oasis is offering is practically a death sentence for the library." She explained that their funding was tied to how many people used the library. "If our patrons can't get to us, we won't be able to keep our doors open."

"Do you have any other ideas?" Vicki asked.

"There are other sites in West Heights that Oasis owns that are sitting there, empty. Why not lease one of those to us instead?"

"Most of those have been earmarked for future development. The ones that aren't are far too valuable to lease to a library."

"Then give us more time to figure something out," April said. "We can try to fundraise enough money for a better location or think of an alternative."

"Look," Vicki said. "Oasis is already behind on the Oakmont Street project. We can't afford to put it off anymore. We can't give you any longer than the 90 days you were already given."

"Then what was the point of this?" April's voice rose. "Why did you agree to meet me if you were just going to tell me the same thing again?"

"Because I thought you were going to suggest something reasonable." Vicki finished her drink in one long sip. "We're not a charity."

April clenched her fists, her fingernails digging into the heels of her palms. "So that's what it comes down to for you? Making money no matter the consequences?"

"It's just business."

April stood up, shaking her head. "Here I was, thinking we could work things out. That you actually had a heart and cared about helping the library. I was so wrong." April had tried to be civil. She had tried not to let her feelings control her. But she couldn't contain herself any longer. "You don't give a damn about anyone or anything other than yourself. I hate you, and Oasis, and everything you stand for."

Vicki looked up at April from her chair, somehow still managing to seem like she was looking down on her. "We both know that's not true."

April fumed. "I'm sick of your presumptions. You don't know how I feel."

"Yes, I do. You don't hate me, not really. You don't hate me because I'm working for Oasis. You don't even hate me because you think I'm selfish." Vicki stood up, facing April. "You hate that I'm the only person who can give you what you crave. And you hate that what you want more than anything is to submit to me."

April's skin began to burn. She was certain her red face betrayed the fact that Vicki had hit a nerve. It didn't matter. Because April had Vicki's measure too.

"Maybe you're right," April said. "But I've figured something out. You want my submission just as much as I want to submit to you." She leaned across the table and spoke into Vicki's ear. "I'm the one who is choosing to give it to you. So which of us is really in control here?" Without giving Vicki a chance to reply, April picked up her purse and strode out of the room.

April left the building more determined than ever. Although the meeting had been a disaster, it hadn't been a waste of time. It had proved something important to April —she couldn't rely on Vicki's help with the library. Moreover, she and Vicki were on opposite sides of this fight.

If April wanted to save her library, she would have to do it herself.

That night, she sent Vicki her photo at exactly 11:59 p.m.

CHAPTER TWELVE

"Is everything okay with you?" Lexi asked April.

The two of them were sitting at a table in a small Mexican restaurant down the street from the library. It used to serve authentic Mexican food, but it had changed ownership about a year ago. Now, it sold 100% organic fusion dishes that tasted nowhere near as good as the old food. However, April and Lexi still came here after work sometimes to chat over dinner.

But for the past ten minutes, April had been so deep in thought that she barely heard a word Lexi said.

"I have a lot on my mind, that's all," April said. "It's fine."

"Are you sure?" Lexi asked. "You seem distracted lately. I know you're taking everything with the library pretty hard, but is that all that's going on?"

April looked down at her plate, avoiding her friend's eyes. She and Lexi usually told each other everything, but she couldn't possibly tell Lexi about what was going on between her and Vicki. Lexi had made her disdain for Vicki clear. Besides, April didn't even understand what was going on between them herself. Just when she was beginning to make sense of their unusual relationship, Vicki would throw her another curve-ball.

You don't hate me. You hate that I'm the only person who can give you what you crave.

"I think I know what's bothering you," Lexi said.

April's heart skipped a beat. "You do?"

"It's about Eliza, isn't it?" Lexi said. "I heard that she's moving away. I know the two of you are close."

"Yeah, you're right."

April hoped that Lexi hadn't seen through her lie. And she really was upset about Eliza leaving too. She felt a twinge of guilt. She hadn't spoken to Eliza since the day she had told April she was leaving. April needed to apologize to her for running off.

She sighed. "Between Eliza leaving, and the library, I feel like all the constants in my life are disappearing."

"Well, there's one thing you can be certain of," Lexi said. "I'm not going anywhere."

April smiled. "Thanks, Lex." It was true. Even though Lexi could be flippant at times, she was always there when April really needed her. "Anyway, I can't do anything about Eliza leaving, but I can do something about the library. I've decided it's time we took matters into our own hands."

"Sounds like you have a plan," Lexi said.

"I don't have one yet, but I'm working on it. My meeting with Vicki made it clear that we're not going to get anywhere with Oasis." April scrunched up her napkin in her fist. "I can't stand that woman."

"I know," Lexi replied. "You've said that ten times today."

"She just drives me crazy! And she thinks she knows everything—"

"Can we *please* stop talking about Vicki fucking Blake? I'm sick of hearing her name."

"Sorry," April said sheepishly. "I have been talking about her a lot."

"*Anyway*," Lexi said. "When you come up with a plan for the library, let me know, and I'll do what I can."

"Sure. I'm going to need all the help I can get."

Lexi pushed her empty plate away. "I should head home. I have to go get ready for my date."

"The girl from The Sapphire Room?" April asked.

"*A* girl from The Sapphire Room. Not the same one as before."

April shook her head. "Of course not."

They paid the bill and went their separate ways. Instead of going home, April headed to Eliza's. As she enjoyed the cool night air, she made a note to ask Eliza if she had any ideas about how to save the library.

But first, she needed to apologize.

April reached Eliza's house and knocked on the door.

Eliza answered with a smile and invited her in. "I'm about to make some tea, want some?"

"Sure," April said. She sat down at the kitchen table. "I'm sorry about last time I was here. I shouldn't have stormed out like that."

"That's okay," Eliza said. "I know you didn't mean anything by it. You were upset."

"That's still no excuse. It was rude. I'm sorry."

"It's fine, don't worry about it. I'm sure it was a shock to hear that I'm leaving after all this time. It was a shock to me as well."

Eliza brought the tea over to the table and handed a cup to April. April inhaled the faintly floral scent. It was calming.

"I've been thinking about moving in with my sister since my diagnosis," Eliza said. "It makes more sense than my living here by myself. But I'm going to miss this place. And West Heights, and all the people who live here."

"We're going to miss you too," April said.

Eliza continued to fill April in on her plans. The sale of her house had just gone through, and she would be moving in a month or so. To April, a month seemed too short.

"That's enough about me," Eliza said. "I hear you're in talks with the woman from Oasis. How's that going?"

April recounted the events of both her meetings with Vicki. "And in the end, all she had to say was 'it's just business.' That's all she cares about. Money."

"All *she* cares about?" Eliza asked. "Is it Oasis you're mad at, or Vicki?"

April folded her arms on her chest. "As far as I'm concerned, they're one and the same."

"You know that's not true. She doesn't deserve to be the target of your anger. She's just one woman trying to do her job. You're always so quick to see the world as black and white, good and evil. There are shades of gray."

"Maybe you're right." Once again, April was letting her feelings about Vicki cloud her judgment. Was it unrealistic of her to try to keep their two worlds separate?

It didn't matter. Right now, April had a more important problem to deal with.

"It's obvious that Oasis isn't open to negotiation," she said. "I'm trying to come up with some other way to save the library, but I'm out of ideas." April recounted everything they'd already tried, from sending out letters to the library's regular donors, to submitting a signed petition to the mayor.

"Maybe you need to cast a wider net," Eliza said.

"What do you mean?"

"My sister was telling me about how a middle school in Seattle was being shut down and combined with a high school halfway across the city. The students and teachers started a petition online to stop it. It was shared all over the internet, and they got thousands of signatures. And it worked. All the negative publicity meant that the school board was forced to rescind the proposal."

"Huh." April had already started an online fundraising page. Maybe she needed to think bigger.

"Could you do what they did?" Eliza asked. "Mobilize the wider community online, really get the attention of Oasis and everyone involved with the project?"

"That's not a bad idea."

April sipped her tea thoughtfully. Eliza was on the right track. But April was going to do far more than an online petition. She was going to turn the entire city against Oasis Developments.

Vicki wouldn't know what hit her.

CHAPTER THIRTEEN

The following Monday, April had barely returned from her lunch break when Vicki came storming into the office at the back of the library. She was closely followed by the head librarian, who mouthed April a silent apology before scurrying off.

Vicki marched up to April's desk. "What the hell did you do?"

April suppressed a smile. "What do you mean?"

"You know exactly what I mean," Vicki said.

April turned to Lexi, who was sitting at her desk, making a half-hearted effort to look like she wasn't listening. "Do you mind, Lexi?" April didn't like to kick Lexi out of her own office, but she knew that things were about to get heated.

"No problem, boss. I'll go grab a coffee." Lexi got up and left the room, shooting Vicki a withering look on the way out.

"Well?" Vicki asked.

"Well, what?" April said.

"I don't have time for this. This stunt you pulled? Do you have any idea how much trouble you've caused me?"

The stunt that Vicki was referring to? April had taken Eliza's advice. Not only had she started an online petition to save the library, but she'd started a campaign to make it go viral.

Well, it was mostly Lexi. April didn't know much about social media, but Lexi, who ran a popular blog about the city's music scene, was an expert. They made a short video about the library and the important role it played in the community, complete with heart-wrenching testimonies from community members the shutdown would affect. An eccentric historian who spoke about the building's past. A sweet old grandma who moved to America from rural Chile and had learned to speak English because of the library's free lessons. An adorable third grader whose parents couldn't afford to buy her books, so she came to the library every single day. It felt a little exploitative to April, but she had to do whatever she could to achieve her goal.

It worked. Lexi had shared the video with her huge network of friends. She knew everyone, including other bloggers and social media stars. Within a few days, the video had been viewed and shared thousands of times, and the petition had thousands of signatures. The fundraising page they had started months ago had gotten a surge in donations. It was nowhere near enough to save the library. But it was better than nothing.

And the best part? Half the city seemed to have turned against Oasis Developments. Oasis, and companies like them, had been doing similar things in other parts of the city for years, and people weren't happy about it. April had no doubt that their PR department was in damage control. She hadn't even considered the fact that it would directly affect Vicki's job.

But any sympathy she had for Vicki quickly evaporated.

"Do you have any idea how much this has cost me?" Vicki said. "Because of you, everything I've worked for is in jeopardy!"

"Do you really think you're the victim in all this?" April asked. "Oasis Developments, and companies just like them have been pushing people out and destroying communities for far too long. This backlash? It's what you deserve."

"So this is about revenge to you?"

"Of course not. I'm not that petty. It's about saving the Oakmont Street Library."

"I've seen your little fundraiser," Vicki said. "Do you really think a few thousand dollars is going to make a difference?"

"It's not about the money," April said. "It's about putting pressure on Oasis. And you've made it clear that Oasis is feeling the pressure right now."

"You're delusional. I've said it before, there's nothing you can do to stop this." Vicki shook her head. "Why did I even try to help you?"

"I don't know why you bothered either, considering how inadequate your help has been. Which is why I had to take action."

"You're not going to give this up, are you?"

April crossed her arms. "Nope."

Vicki let out an irritated sigh. "The very moment that we met, I knew you were going to be trouble. I should have listened to my instincts. You've been a thorn in my side since day one."

"Don't you remember what you told me the night that we met?" April asked innocently. "You said that you like a challenge."

Vicki planted her hands on the desk and leaned down until her face was inches from April's. "You can't help yourself, can you? You just keep pushing and pushing. It's like everything you do is designed to infuriate me."

April's breath caught in her chest. Although Vicki hadn't raised her voice, her tone was overpowering. And her eyes smoldered. Not with anger, or annoyance.

With passion.

April held Vicki's gaze. At that moment, she wanted Vicki to push her against the desk and do exactly what she had threatened to do that day in her office.

Instead, Vicki turned on her heel and walked toward the door.

"Wait," April said.

Vicki stopped. "What is it?"

April whipped her phone out and sent a message to Vicki. It was a photo she'd taken that morning.

Vicki's phone pinged in her jacket pocket. She pulled it out, glanced at the screen, then slipped it back into her pocket without looking at the message.

"Saving it for later, are you?" April asked.

Vicki shot April a blazing look. "Oh, the things I want to do to you," she said softly. Then without another word, Vicki left the room.

April blew out a breath. She didn't know what she was thinking, provoking Vicki like that at work. Their pretense of keeping business and pleasure separate had been thrown out the window in Vicki's office the other day. However, that didn't mean it was a good idea to ignore the lines they had wordlessly drawn.

A few minutes later, Lexi returned to the room. "Did you and Vicki have a nice chat?" she asked.

"It went about how you'd expect," April replied.

"I wish you hadn't kicked me out. I would have loved to watch you take her on."

April remembered the glare Lexi gave Vicki on her way out. "You really don't like her, do you? What did she ever do to you?"

"Nothing. I just don't like her or the way she treats people, that's all." Lexi said hurriedly. She sat down at her desk. "I better get to work. I have a bunch of calls to make about the charity ball."

That was one part of April's old event coordinator job that she didn't miss. Every year, the library teamed up with a local literacy charity and a private association made of wealthy old ladies to throw a fundraising ball. And every year, it had gotten more and more extravagant. It was a nightmare to organize. To top it off, the event coordinator had to attend the ball to make sure everything ran smoothly. April was just glad she didn't have to go this year.

Still, April sympathized with her friend. "Let me know if you need any help," she said.

Lexi muttered a thanks. "I'll be glad when it's over. Then I can go back to organizing author visits and poetry nights."

April had just as much to do as Lexi. Although Lexi had done most of the work setting up the library's viral campaign, April had taken it over. And it had blown up to the point where it was becoming unmanageable. The library's social media accounts were abuzz with activity. The library had its own hashtag, and people were sending messages of support. It was encouraging to see the community rallying around the library.

Well, most of the community. Apparently, April's campaign had caused a stir in city hall. According to Lexi, who was on top of all the gossip, the Mayor wasn't too happy about how April's campaign made the Mayor and the rest of the city council look. After all, they supported the Oakmont Street development, and had made no effort to help the library. April had about as much sympathy for them as she did for Oasis.

She spent the rest of the day responding to emails and inquiries about the library. Journalists were calling her for quotes, and she had been asked to write an editorial for an online newspaper. A national news station wanted to interview her for a piece on the corporate takeover of historic neighborhoods all over the country. April hadn't meant for things to blow up this much, but she was glad they had. Maybe it would actually make a difference.

By the time five p.m. rolled around, April was wiped out. She could deal with the rest at home. As she got up to leave, her phone buzzed. She unlocked it and read the message. It was from Vicki.

Tomorrow night. 9 p.m. My apartment.

CHAPTER FOURTEEN

*A*pril knocked on the door to Vicki's apartment. She'd barely had time to go home between finishing work and coming here. Today had been as busy as the day before.

April couldn't help but feel smug. She had finally gotten one up on Vicki. But she may have taken things too far in her office yesterday. That look Vicki had given her before leaving made her wonder if Vicki was finally going to do something about April's misbehavior. April's mind raced with possibilities, each more deliciously twisted than the last.

April knocked again. What was taking Vicki so long? It was just past nine p.m., so April wasn't early. She waited for a few more minutes, then tried the door handle. It was unlocked.

April stepped inside, shutting the door behind her. "Vicki?"

She was met with silence.

April looked around, frowning. A few lights were on, but

Vicki was nowhere to be seen. Sebastian sat on his perch on the arm of the couch, nothing more than a silhouette in the dim light.

"Where the hell is she?" April asked. *Great, now I'm talking to a cat.*

In response, Sebastian gave her a disdainful stare before slinking off into another room.

April made her way to Vicki's bedroom and poked her head through the door. "Vicki?"

Vicki wasn't in the bedroom either, but it was clear that this was where April was supposed to be. The room was almost completely dark, but the doors of the large closet were flung open, the built-in lights illuminating Vicki's collection of BDSM equipment and toys. And in the center of the rug in front of the bed was a single chair.

April walked over to the chair. A strip of dark red fabric hung over the back, and there was a piece of paper folded in half on the seat. April picked it up. It was a handwritten note with three instructions.

Sit down.

Put the blindfold on.

Wait.

April's pulse began to race. What was Vicki playing at? She glanced at the door behind her. There was still no sign of Vicki.

April took in a breath and sat down on the chair. Taking one last look at the cupboard full of toys, she wrapped the strip of fabric over her eyes and tied it securely behind her head.

She sat back and waited. Was Vicki in the house somewhere, out of sight? It occurred to April that she should have checked the rest of the house before sitting down and blindfolding herself. That would have been the logical thing to do.

Hell, anything other than this would have been the logical thing to do. April had gone into Vicki's empty apartment and served herself up on a platter. Vicki, a woman she'd royally screwed over the day before. Vicki, who owned a large collection of kinky torture tools. Vicki, whose idea of a good time was spanking someone into obedience.

Oh, the things I want to do to you...

Something creaked behind April's chair. A footstep? She listened carefully but couldn't hear anything more. She breathed in and caught a whiff of Vicki's perfume. That didn't mean much. April was in Vicki's bedroom—her scent was on everything.

April waited a few more minutes. At least, it felt like minutes, but she had no way of knowing. Alone and blindfolded, with nothing but silence to keep her company, time seemed to pass excruciatingly slowly.

Suddenly, April felt a gust of air breeze past her. "Vicki?" she called out.

Again, the only answer was silence.

"This is crazy," April muttered. Why was she doing this? She should just get up and walk away, stop playing this silly game, no matter how much it turned her on.

A few more minutes passed, and April decided she'd had enough. She stood up and reached behind her head to untie the blindfold.

"Giving up so soon?" Vicki's voice emerged from the darkness.

April jumped. "How long have you been here?"

Vicki didn't answer.

"Victoria!"

Still, Vicki said nothing.

April sighed. Then she sat back down and dropped her hands to her lap.

"That's better," Vicki said from behind her. "Hands behind your back."

"Are you going to tie them up?" April asked.

"Hands behind your back." Vicki placed her hands on April's shoulders.

As soon as Vicki touched her, April's frustration dissipated, only to be replaced by anxious excitement. She crossed her hands behind the back of the chair. Immediately, Vicki's hands were at her wrists, tying a thick, soft rope around them.

When Vicki was done, April tugged at her bonds experimentally. Her wrists were bound both to each other and the back of the chair itself. And with her hands tied, April couldn't remove the blindfold.

She was at Vicki's mercy. There was nothing she wanted more.

Vicki rounded the chair to stand in front of April. "Are you comfortable?" she asked.

"What do you think?" April said.

Vicki swept her hand down April's cheek, her fingertips whispering across April's skin. "I've had enough of your games. Bending my rules, defying me at every turn, trying to get under my skin. Do you have any idea how much you've been driving me crazy?"

April smiled. "I drive you crazy, do I? Make you lose control?"

Vicki took April's chin and tilted her head up. "What did I say about talking back to me?" Vicki's warm breath tickled April's ear.

"That you like it?"

Vicki spoke in a soft growl. "Be. Quiet."

"Make me," April whispered.

At once, Vicki's lips were on April's, kissing her with a ferocity that stunned her into silence. April dissolved into the chair beneath her, every inch of her ablaze.

Vicki tore herself away. "You're going to sit there quietly while I remind you of who you belong to."

A thrill rippled through April's body. That kiss alone was enough to remind April of who she belonged to. It reminded her of why she had been drawn to Vicki in the first place, why she came back to Vicki time and time again, despite everything. Why she always yielded to Vicki in the end.

Vicki slid her hands down April's chest and grabbed the front of her top. She pulled it down, exposing April's breasts. Her fingers grazed April's nipples, causing them to tighten into tiny peaks. Vicki pinched them in her fingertips.

April moaned. That night at Lilith's Den seemed to have flicked a switch in her brain that made pain and pleasure blend and amplify each other in the most delicious way. Vicki trailed her lips down April's chest and sucked her other nipple between her teeth. April bucked in the chair, a cry escaping her.

"Didn't I tell you to keep quiet?" Vicki said.

April bit her lip. Did Vicki really expect April to stay silent while she ravished her like this? Vicki's demanding hands and mouth roamed all over April's chest, her shoulders, her neck. She was like a woman possessed, so consumed with lust that she couldn't hold herself back. April felt the same way, but with her hands bound and her eyes blindfolded, she couldn't do anything except let Vicki have her way.

Vicki slipped her hand down to where April's thighs met. Even through her jeans, Vicki's touch inflamed her.

Vicki leaned in, her lips grazing April's cheek. "This right here? This is mine. Your body is mine. Your pleasure is mine. You. Are. Mine."

April's skin prickled. At the back of her mind, April felt like she shouldn't want this. To belong to anyone, especially not Vicki. But that part of her was drowned out by her overwhelming desire to relinquish everything to Vicki.

Vicki drew her hands up to April's waist and unbuttoned her jeans. She yanked them down April's legs, taking her now-soaking panties with them.

"Open your legs," Vicki said.

April obeyed, her whole body pulsing with anticipation. Vicki ran her hands down April's sides and grabbed her ass cheeks, her nails digging into them. She dragged April's hips forward so that her ass was balanced at the edge of the chair. Then Vicki's fingers were between April's thighs, probing at her slick folds.

April quivered. Mercifully, Vicki didn't tease her. She simply buried her fingers inside April and began to fuck her right there on the chair.

"Oh god…" April closed her eyes, her head tipping back.

Vicki's fingers filled her so completely that it was like the other woman was made for her. Every thrust made her shudder and gasp.

April panted and pulled at her bonds, heat flooding her entire body. Vicki was unrelenting. She had one goal, and one goal only—to demonstrate that her possession of April was so complete that she could make April come undone in seconds.

Seconds was all it took.

A fiery orgasm ripped through April's body, the culmination of all the friction they had been feeling toward each other for so long. As April rode it out, Vicki pressed her lips against April's in an urgent, possessive kiss.

* * *

April and Vicki lay in bed, draped lazily across each other. They had spent the last hour working off the tension that lingered between them until both of them were too exhausted to move.

April let out a sigh. It was nice, being wrapped up in Vicki's arms, soaking into Vicki's skin. All the animosity she'd been feeling toward the woman had dissipated. Instead, she felt comfortable and serene. April didn't quite understand why she always felt this way after she and Vicki played their intimate games. Maybe it was a side effect of the vulnerability they shared by exposing the deepest, darkest parts of themselves.

April examined Vicki's face. Up close she could see all the different golden tones in her hair, and each individual hair in Vicki's eyelashes. They were long and fine, and much darker than her hair.

"What is it?" Vicki murmured.

"Nothing," April replied.

Vicki brushed her fingers through her hair, frowning. Her unexpected self-consciousness made April smile. The woman who had tied April to the chair earlier had been replaced by someone a little less imposing.

April reached out to sweep her hand over the mound of Vicki's hip and the valley of her waist. "The other day, in your office, you asked me why I care so much about the library. Why do you want to know?"

"I want to understand you," Vicki said.

"I'll tell you," April said. "But I want to know something in exchange."

Vicki raised an eyebrow. "For a submissive, you're very demanding."

April shrugged. "Those are my terms."

Vicki shook her head. "All right. What do you want to know?"

"I want to know why your job means so much to you," April said. "I want to know who you need to prove yourself to."

For a moment, April thought Vicki was going to clam up. Then she rolled onto her back and looked up at the ceiling.

"That ugly metal thing on the table in my office?" Vicki said. "It was my father's, but he didn't give it to me. He loved that thing, he'd never give it away. I stole it from his study the last time I was home. That was almost ten years ago."

"You haven't been home in ten years?" April asked.

"I haven't wanted to go home. And even if I did, I have

no idea if my parents would even allow me to walk through the door. I'm the black sheep of the family."

"Seriously?" To April, Vicki seemed like Little Miss Perfect.

"I was never the daughter they wanted me to be," Vicki said. "They wanted someone like my younger sister. She married the son of one of my father's business partners and has popped out three perfect little grandchildren. Me? I never wanted that life. When I was younger, I naively wanted to work for my family's company, to take it over one day. I was smart enough for it. But because I don't have the right plumbing, that honor will go to my little brother. So, there's that. And there's the fact that I'm a lesbian. On top of liking women, I've never conformed to my parents' ideas of how a woman should present, even when I was a young girl."

Suddenly, April felt guilty for assuming Vicki had it easy all her life. She knew all too well that the world could be a cruel place for kids who were different. April reached out and stroked Vicki's arm. She felt the other woman relax slightly at her touch.

"My parents did everything they could to try to change me," Vicki said. "Shoving me into dresses. Trying to set me up with their friends' sons as soon as I hit my teens. Once, they made me meet with some religious nutter who claimed he was a psychologist and said he could 'cure' me. In the end, I kicked up enough of a fuss that they never tried that again.

"After that, I went to college on the other side of the country," Vicki continued. "When I came back, I decided I'd had enough, and that I needed to find my own path. When I told my father, he cut me off. He told me I was a perverted, ungrateful brat who was never going to amount to anything. He said I was crazy for even trying."

"That's awful," April said.

"There was a silver lining. My father's words motivated me to prove him wrong. I had some money of my own tucked way, an inheritance from my grandparents that my father couldn't touch. It got me through business school, but after that, I needed to find a job. I looked for a position where I could put my degrees to use, only to find that my father had effectively blacklisted me. No one wanted to hire Harold Blake's renegade daughter.

"That was until I reached out to Oasis," Vicki said. "They're one of my father's biggest rivals. They offered me a job that was well below my qualifications, but I was desperate, so I took it. It wouldn't surprise me if they only hired me to annoy my father, but I was determined to show them I was worth more. So, I worked my ass off until management noticed me and gave me a promotion. And then another, and another, and so on, and here I am."

Vicki folded her hands behind her head. "Sure, I had an easy start to life in most respects. I had every possible opportunity available to me. But my career at Oasis? I earned it through my own hard work. The promotion I'm up for is a chief operations officer position at our head office in Boston. When the CEO retires in a few years time, as COO I'll be next in line. And I'll finally be able to say to my father, and my family, and myself that I'm capable of succeeding without them. That's why this job is so important to me."

"Vicki," April said. "Your family… how could they?"

A faint smile played on Vicki's lips. "You're a real bleeding heart, aren't you? Don't feel bad for me. Everything with my family is in the past. It doesn't bother me anymore. Every so often we run into each other, and I'm reminded of how much better off I am without them."

April couldn't help but wonder if it was April that Vicki was trying to convince, or herself.

"Now it's your turn. Why is this library of yours so important?"

"It's hard to explain." April sat up in the bed, tucking her knees under her chin. "The library is my sanctuary. Well, not so much now. But I used to go there a lot as a teenager."

Before April could elaborate, Vicki's phone started ringing on the nightstand. Vicki glanced over at it.

"Shouldn't you get that?" April asked.

"Let me check who it is." Vicki rolled over and grabbed her phone, then groaned. "It's Oasis head office. They never call this late unless it's an emergency. I should take this," she said apologetically.

April nodded. "Go ahead."

Vicki got up from the bed, wrapped a robe around herself, and walked out of the bedroom.

April stretched out her arms and made her way to the bathroom. She could hear Vicki's voice faintly from the living room. As she washed her hands and fixed her tousled hair in the mirror, she thought back to everything Vicki had shared with her. All along, she had seen Vicki as this privileged snob who had everything in life handed to her. She was starting to wonder if she had Vicki all wrong.

When April returned to the bedroom, Vicki was waiting

for her, phone in hand. "I need to take care of something," she said. "This might take a while."

"I should head home anyway," April replied. She was hoping to go into the library early in the morning to get a start on all the work she had to do.

With a nod, Vicki disappeared back into the living room. April got dressed and left the bedroom. She found Vicki sitting on the couch, her laptop open on the coffee table, the phone to her ear. One bare leg poked out of her robe.

As April approached the door, Sebastian appeared out of nowhere at April's feet, weaving himself around April's legs.

Seriously? Now that I'm leaving, you decide to get friendly? As she reached down to pet him, he darted away and went to curl up on Vicki's lap.

Sighing, April waved goodbye to Vicki and slipped out.

She smiled to herself. Despite everything that was going on, she and Vicki seemed to have come to a tentative understanding. It made her wonder. If it wasn't for everything with the library, would things between them be different?

April pushed the thought out of her mind. It could never work, for so many reasons. Besides, it was a dangerous line of thinking. The reality was that they were still working against each other.

April could never forget that they were at opposite sides of this fight.

CHAPTER FIFTEEN

*L*exi slammed down the phone and let out a heavy sigh.

"Everything okay, Lex?" April asked.

"It's the caterers for the ball on the weekend," Lexi said. "They can't get ahold of the company that's supplying the ice sculptures. This is ridiculous! Why do we even need ice sculptures?"

"You know how it is," April said. "The more extravagant the event is, the more we can charge for tickets. And the more people will donate."

"I have an idea. Why don't we skip the ball altogether and donate the money from the funds we'd save instead?"

"I don't think the association that's funding the ball would go for that. Those rich old ladies need an excuse to throw a party."

"Then they should organize it themselves," Lexi grumbled. "I wish we could throw one of these parties to raise funds for the library."

"If only we weren't so pressed for time," April said.

"These things take all year to organize. Plus, we need the money to fund an event like that in the first place." She sighed. "At least the online fundraiser is going strong."

After April's TV interview, things had picked up. Apparently, she had started a discussion, and people from West Heights and the rest of the city were weighing in with their opinions. And April herself was getting a lot of attention. Friends and strangers had even sent her messages of support.

She opened up her social media page to check on things, and groaned. "Not again."

"What's the matter?" Lexi asked.

"People keep leaving hateful comments. First, it was on the library page, and now it's on my page too. Look at this one. 'You should be grateful that Oasis is cleaning up all the trash that lives in West Heights.' And it just gets worse from there. Who is this person and why do they care so much?"

"Ugh." Lexi screwed up her face. "It must be some online troll. I get them on my blog all the time. They seem to get off on harassing people, all while hiding behind the anonymity of a computer screen."

"That's messed up," April said.

"Welcome to the internet, where people can be assholes without consequences." Lexi came over to April's desk and pointed to a little red button at the corner of her screen. "You can report the comments and block him."

April clicked the button and sent off a report. "This isn't even the worst of it. Just yesterday, someone posted a misogynistic tirade on my page. It barely even had anything to do with the library! I don't understand how people can be so nasty."

Lexi squeezed April's shoulder. "Are you going to be all right? Do you want me to take over the social media stuff for you?"

"It's okay," April said. She was a grown woman. She wasn't going to let some online bullies get to her. "I can handle it."

"Let me know if you change your mind," Lexi said. "In the meantime, I'm going to grab a coffee before the meeting with Vicki."

Right. April had been so distracted by the unsettling comments that she'd forgotten all about it. After April's TV interview, Oasis had backpedaled, stating that they were still negotiating with the library representatives. The next day, Vicki's assistant called April to arrange another meeting. She didn't give any details, but April was hopeful.

"I'll see you there," she said to Lexi.

Five minutes later, April got up and headed to the meeting room. It was all the way at the other end of the building, and she got lost in her thoughts as she walked.

"Hi, April."

April jumped, her hand flying up to her chest. "Vicki. You scared me." The blonde-haired woman stood next to her, that irritatingly sexy smile on her face.

"I haven't gotten my photo yet today," Vicki said.

April shushed her and glanced around. They were alone. "You'll get it when I'm ready." She continued toward the meeting room.

Vicki placed her hand at the small of April's back. "You know I don't like to wait."

Heat spread up April's cheeks. "What would happen if I didn't send you a picture?"

"Try it and find out."

One look at Vicki's face told April that she wasn't messing around. It only tempted April more. One of these days, she was going to test whether Vicki would actually follow through on her threats. But not today. She had already taken a photo, she was just waiting for the right moment to send it.

Just before they came into view of the meeting room, Vicki pulled her hand away. April's back tingled where Vicki had touched her.

"After you." Vicki opened the door.

April and Vicki entered the room and took their places at opposite ends of the table. They were the last to arrive. Lexi gave April a strange look. April avoided her gaze.

"Sorry we're late," Vicki said. "April and I were having a very interesting conversation."

April ignored Vicki's comment. "Let's get started." Surreptitiously, she placed her phone in her lap and tapped the screen, sending off a message.

Right on cue, Vicki pulled out her phone and glanced at it under the table. Her gaze flicked up to April, the thirst in her eyes hidden from all but April.

"Vicki?" April said. "You called the meeting, is there something you'd like to share with us?"

"Yes." Vicki shoved her phone in her pocket and cleared her throat. "Given the recent attention that the Oakmont Street Library has been getting in the media, Oasis Developments has decided it's in everyone's best interests to delay the Oakmont Street project until a more suitable location for the library can be found."

April's heart leaped. *It worked. It actually worked.* "That's great," she said. The library wasn't safe just yet, but this was the best outcome they could have hoped for. Now they had enough time to figure out what to do.

"I've been talking to the head of our corporate sponsorship program, and he's going to see if we can spare some funds," Vicki said. "It won't be much, but it should help."

"That would be amazing," April said.

"I understand you've been doing some fundraising," Vicki said.

"Yes. And now that we have more time, we can raise even more. And there are some federal grants we can apply for."

The two of them went back and forth, discussing options, the others around the table chiming in now and then. Vicki took plenty of notes and seemed to be taking their feedback and suggestions seriously.

Almost an hour later, the meeting came to an end. As everyone filed out of the room, April told Lexi she'd catch up with her, and stayed in her seat. April didn't have to ask Vicki to stay. Once the room had emptied, Vicki sat down next to April.

"So, what do you think?" she asked.

"This is amazing!" April said. "Why didn't you tell me about it sooner?"

"It wasn't a done deal until this morning. I had to get approval from the board. They weren't exactly pleased with my proposition, but I convinced them that going forward now would be a PR disaster."

"*You* did this?"

"What can I say? You're a tenacious woman. You wore me down."

"Vicki, thank you!"

April beamed. She was so happy, she wanted to throw her arms around Vicki's neck and kiss her, to run her fingers through those blonde locks, to bury herself in Vicki's skin.

But the room they were in had glass walls and everyone could see them. Already, they were sitting much too close.

"I should get going," April said. "I have so much work to do."

"So do I," Vicki replied. "I've been putting out fires all week because of your little campaign."

"I hope you're not expecting an apology."

"I'm not. Even I have to admit, it was a smart play. I'd be commending you if I wasn't the target of this. You should be working PR at a Fortune 500 company."

"I would never take a job like that in a million years," April said.

"Of course you wouldn't," Vicki said. "You're too busy crusading for the greater good. Your talents are wasted here."

"There's nowhere else I'd rather be."

The two of them gathered their things and left the room.

"I'll see you later." April was uncertain of whether it was a question or a statement.

"Oh, I'll be seeing you," Vicki said. "As soon as everything cools down, you're coming to my apartment, and I'm going to give you a taste of the rest of my collection." She straightened up her blazer. "By the way, that picture you sent me. Did you take it at your desk?"

"I did," April replied.

Vicki shook her head. "You're a bold woman." With that, she turned and headed for the exit.

April made her way back to her office. It was almost five p.m., and it was Friday. All the excitement of the week had been taxing. April wanted nothing more than to go home and have a long soak in the bath. She was looking forward to doing absolutely nothing for the entire weekend.

When April reached her office, Lexi was sitting with her feet up on her desk and her arms crossed.

She gave April a cold look. "Have a nice talk with Vicki, did you?"

"I don't know what you mean," April replied.

"I thought you hated her. Now the two of you are acting like best friends?"

"We're working together. I'm just being friendly. It's nothing more than that." April didn't like lying to her friend, but Lexi had made her feelings about Vicki very clear. "What do you have against her, anyway? Did she try to steal some girl you were chasing?"

"Like I said, I don't like the way she treats women," Lexi replied.

"That has nothing to do with our jobs and the library. You're being unfair."

"You're actually defending her now? Unbelievable." Lexi muttered something else under her breath that April didn't catch.

"I don't understand why you're so angry," April said.

"I'm angry because you're falling for her act." Lexi picked up her bag and grabbed her coat. "Vicki Blake can't be trusted. She's just going to end up screwing us over." Without another word, Lexi stormed out of the office.

CHAPTER SIXTEEN

April was woken up on Saturday morning by the ringing of her phone. She rolled over and picked it up. It was Lexi. The two of them hadn't spoken since Lexi stormed out of their office the day before. April wasn't upset with her. The two of them had been friends for years, and they were both hot-tempered. It wasn't the first time they'd had a disagreement.

April answered the phone. "Hi, Lex."

"April," Lexi said. "Look, I'm sorry about yesterday. I was just in a bad mood, and I took it out on you."

"It's all right."

"No, it's not. I was being a jerk."

"Seriously, it's fine. God knows how many times you've had to put up with my bad moods." April frowned. "Is everything else okay? You don't sound too good."

"I don't feel too good," Lexi said. "I think I ate something bad last night. I've been up since four a.m. puking into a bucket."

"Are you all right?"

"I'll live," Lexi replied. "Look, I hate to apologize then ask for a favor, but I don't have any other options."

"Sure, what do you need?" April asked.

"The charity ball is tonight. I can't go like this. Do you think you could go in my place? Please?"

April stifled a groan. The charity ball wasn't her idea of a good time. The giant party was always full of insanely wealthy people who had more money than sense and spent the whole night getting dangerously intoxicated.

But she couldn't say no to Lexi. "Sure," April said. "I'll do it." It wasn't like she had anything better to do with her Saturday night.

"Thank you so much," Lexi said. "I promise you won't have to do much. There shouldn't be any surprises, but you can call me if you need help and I'll do what I can."

"Don't worry about it. I've organized these things before, remember? Just rest up." April walked over to her closet. She would have to find something to wear. Even though she intended to spend most of her time hiding behind the scenes, she would stand out unless she was in formal wear.

"You're the best, April," Lexi said.

"You owe me. Next time we get dinner after work, you're buying."

"Done. By the way, there's a theme this year," Lexi said. "You're going to need a mask."

April pulled off her black-and-red eye mask. She had borrowed it from Lexi, and it fit too snugly.

She had to admit, Lexi's idea to make the event a

masquerade ball was a good one. The ball was in full swing now, and the guests seemed to be enjoying themselves even more than usual. Sure, the ball was always one big display of hedonistic excess, but this year was different. It was like some kind of magic spell had been cast on the room, like the act of putting on a mask made everyone lose their inhibitions. It didn't make sense. It wasn't like the flimsy masks everyone was wearing provided any anonymity. Perhaps even adults liked to play pretend sometimes.

At the very least, rich, drunk people were extremely generous, especially in front of their peers. Someone had made a sizable anonymous donation. It was encouraging to know that all the money and effort put into throwing the ball was worth it.

Lexi hadn't lied when she said April wouldn't have to do much. She'd organized everything well, from the band right down to the stunning ice sculptures. Save for keeping an eye out for rowdy guests, and dealing with some technical issues during the speeches, April's night had been an easy one. She only had a couple of hours before she would be back home in bed with a book.

April's stomach rumbled. The ball had been going for hours, and she hadn't eaten anything since she arrived. She spotted a waiter disappearing into the crowd, his tray laden with appetizers. Although she wasn't a guest, no one could blame April for grabbing a few.

April slipped her mask back on and made her way through the crowd in search of the waiter. She attracted the odd stare, no doubt because of her dress. She had made the mistake of wearing a simple, vivid red gown, one that stood out in a sea of black and diamonds. But mostly, she passed through almost invisible, beneath the notice of the upper-class guests.

She found the waiter, grabbed some canapes, then made her way toward some chairs in the corner, stuffing the food into her mouth. As the crowd thinned near the side of the hall, April's eyes landed on a familiar figure, a slender blonde woman leaning against the wall with her hands in her pockets

Vicki.

April froze. She hadn't expected to see Vicki tonight. She wasn't at all prepared for it. Despite everything, April still had a tendency to lose her mind around Vicki. And right now, April was losing her mind just looking at her. Vicki had a flair for rocking suits while still looking utterly feminine. Tonight, she was wearing a fitted black tuxedo, and heels which accentuated her legs and made her look even slimmer. Her soft blonde hair was swept back, and she had a red flower pinned to her lapel. Her mask was a delicate creation of black lace that covered the area around her eyes.

Vicki's eyes met April's, her gaze pinning April in place. April gulped down the rest of her canape as Vicki approached her.

"April." Vicki flashed her a smile. "Don't you look enchanting?"

April's cheeks grew warm. "Vicki. I didn't know you were coming."

"What can I say, I enjoy a nice ball. It's for a good cause after all."

"Do you even know what charity this ball is raising money for?" April asked.

Vicki shrugged. "Something about sick children?"

"Not even close."

"I have to say, you're the last person I'd expect to see here." Vicki's eyes flicked down April's body and back up again. "Not that I'm complaining, of course."

"I'm here on library business," April said. "I'm filling in for Lexi. I should probably get back to work." April didn't actually have anything to do, but being around Vicki while she was looking as devastatingly sexy as she was right now seemed dangerous.

"Wait," Vicki said. "Come mingle with me."

"Mingle? I'm not a guest. And no offense, but this isn't my kind of crowd."

"They're not all bad. Besides, there's something I want to show you."

"What is it?"

"Come with me and you'll find out."

April's curiosity was piqued, but this seemed like a bad idea. "What if someone sees us together? I don't want anyone to think I'm your date. Because of work, I mean," she added hurriedly.

"Nobody knows who you are here," Vicki said. "And everyone is too drunk and self-absorbed to notice you. Besides, between your mask and that wickedly sexy dress you're wearing, even I barely recognized you. You'll just be another face in the crowd." She drew her fingers through her hair. "Who knows, you might even enjoy yourself."

April fidgeted with her mask. It was tempting. To get lost in the crowd with Vicki, to pretend, just for a moment, that they weren't at opposite sides of the battle over the library.

"So? What do you say?" Vicki held out her hand, her eyes

speaking a command April desperately wanted to follow, one she had given April so many times before. *Give in to your desires.*

"Okay," April said. "But only for a little while. Then I'm going back to work."

April took Vicki's hand, and Vicki whisked April away into the crowd. As a waiter passed them, Vicki snatched up a couple of glasses of champagne and handed one to April. "Consider it camouflage."

April sipped the drink, the smooth liquid warming her chest. "This is good." In all the years she'd organized the ball, she'd never actually tried the champagne. She'd never stood in the hall like she was right now, in the midst of all the people, doing nothing but soaking in the glitz and glamor. The grand old hall seemed so alive.

They continued through the crowd, Vicki greeting people here and there. Occasionally, Vicki would stop and chat with some of them about everything from gossip and small talk to business. April couldn't see a pattern to the people Vicki talked to. But they all had too much money and too much power, both of which they threw around thoughtlessly. It only proved to April that these were not her kind of people.

As Vicki had predicted, no one took any notice of April, which was fine with her. She simply stood there silently, sipping champagne, until Vicki dragged her off to talk to someone else.

April was beginning to wonder what the point of all this was when they were approached by a pair of women. One of them, a tall dark-haired woman, looked familiar to her, but her elaborate half mask made it difficult for April to place her.

Vicki greeted them both. "April, this is Mel. You've already met Vanessa."

Right. April had briefly met Vanessa that night at Lilith's Den. The other woman, a slight brunette, was looking at Vicki with an expression on her face that could only be described as hostile. Was this the girlfriend of Vanessa's that Vicki had "caused trouble" for?

"We meet again, April," Vanessa said, shooting Vicki a look.

"I'm not with her," April blurted. "I just mean, we're not-"

"We didn't come together," Vicki clarified. "We just happened to run into each other."

"What a coincidence," Vanessa said.

"I'm actually working tonight," April said. "I run the library that's sponsoring the ball."

"The library on Oakmont Street, right?" Mel asked. "I heard that it's getting shut down. It's too bad. I work for a non-profit legal service downtown. A lot of our clients use the library. It has some great resources."

"Yes, it does," April said. She glanced sideways at Vicki. "It's a real pity."

"It's not being shut down," Vicki said. "The project has been put on hold until everything with the library has been sorted out."

"That's right," Vanessa said. "The Oakmont Street Project is yours, isn't it, Vic?" She looked from Vicki to April. "How interesting."

April sighed. Despite April's protestations, it was clear

that Vanessa didn't believe that nothing was going on between April and Vicki. It didn't help that she had seen them at Lilith's Den together.

Mel, however, didn't share Vanessa's amusement. Her wariness of Vicki was clear on her face. She turned to address April. "Assuming the library is staying open, we should talk about setting up a partnership between the Legal Services Project and the Oakmont Street Library," Mel said. "We're always looking for ways to make it easier for people who need our services to find us."

"That would be amazing," April said. "We get a lot of people coming in to look up legal reference books because they can't afford lawyers."

"Great," Mel said. "I'll be in touch."

"Why don't we leave these two alone?" Vanessa wrapped her arm around Mel's waist. "It was lovely to see you again, April."

Mel said goodbye to April and gave Vicki another withering look before she and Vanessa walked off.

April turned to Vicki. "No one knows me here, huh?"

"I wasn't planning on running into Vanessa," Vicki said.

"And all those other people we've run into? That was intentional?"

"Yes. I'm proving a point."

"Which is?" April asked.

"You'll have to wait and see," Vicki said.

"All this mingling and this mysterious 'something' you want to show me has yet to materialize." April crossed her arms. "I'm starting to suspect you have an ulterior motive."

"Oh? And what would that be?"

"I don't know, to drag me around this party drinking champagne with you?"

Vicki lifted her glass. "You make it sound like such an awful thing."

"Victoria!"

"I was kidding," Vicki said. "I assure you, there's a point to all this. Trust me."

"Okay then," April said. "By the way, what did you do to get on Mel's bad side?"

Vicki waved her hand dismissively. "I made a few harmless comments to her at a ball just like this one, and apparently she took them the wrong way."

Before April could question her further, Vicki's eyes landed on a group of half a dozen people, standing around with drinks in their hands.

"Come on." Vicki held out her arm for April to take. "Try not to lose your temper, okay?"

"What do you mean?" April asked.

Vicki didn't answer her. Instead, she pulled April over to the group, slipping into a gap in the circle.

"Good to see you, Vicki," the woman next to April said. She had straight brown hair and a warm smile, and she looked to be around forty.

"Camilla. This is April," Vicki said. "April, Camilla."

April and Camilla exchanged a brief greeting. As the conversation continued around them, Vicki quietly spoke in April's ear, telling April who everyone was. There was one woman, an older lady, who Vicki simply referred to as 'the Duchess.' Next to her was Senator Williams, who April recognized from TV, and his wife. Everyone looked like they'd had plenty to drink.

When the conversation died down, Camilla addressed Vicki again. "How are things at Oasis? I hear you've been having some trouble with one of your major projects?"

"Yes, the Oakmont Street development in West Heights. The locals are being difficult." Vicki waved her hands dismissively. "They're up in arms because we're 'destroying the neighborhood.'"

The locals? *Difficult?* April couldn't believe what was coming out of Vicki's mouth.

Senator Williams scoffed. "West Heights is prime real estate now, but it's covered in all those ugly old townhouses. They're a waste of valuable space."

"Well, if the locals don't like it, they can move somewhere else," the Duchess said.

April fumed. Did Vicki really expect April to just stand here and listen to these snobs badmouth West Heights? She opened her mouth to retort when Camilla spoke.

"It's unfortunate," she said. "There are some lovely old buildings in the area. Isn't there a museum that's going to be demolished?"

"It's a library," April said sharply.

"Yes, it is a library." Vicki placed a hand on April's shoulder. "April works there."

"Do you, dear?" The Duchess peered at April over her glasses. "It's very generous of you to give up your time like that."

Did this woman think April was some kind of volunteer? Of course, it made a lot more sense than someone who actually had a job at a library being a guest at a party like this. April did look like a guest right now, considering she was walking around with Vicki holding a glass of champagne.

"Yes, she's a real dear, this one," Vicki said, a mocking edge in her voice that only April seemed to notice. "She's been helping Oasis work out a solution to relocate the library."

"Well, I for one don't see the point," the Duchess said. "Do people even use libraries anymore? Can't they just *buy* books?"

"The library isn't just for books," April said. "Plenty of people use libraries for the other resources they offer, like computers and free wifi."

"Don't they have those at home?"

April resisted the urge to roll her eyes. "Some people can't afford them. That's why places like the Oakmont Street Library are so important."

Without thinking, April launched into an impromptu speech about the importance of the library. When she finished, she realized that everyone in the circle was staring at her.

"I had no idea," the Duchess said. "Did you know about this, Vicki?"

"Not until April told me about it," Vicki said.

"Well it sounds like you've got an important thing going there, April," Camilla said. "I'd love to help out. I'm sure I could find some funds to make a donation to the library."

April beamed. "That would be wonderful."

"Yes, I'll speak with my husband about making a contribution," the Duchess said loudly. "He's the Duke of Immingham, you know. We're very charitable people."

Camilla tilted her head toward April and spoke under

her breath. "Good luck getting anything from her. Last I heard, 'the Duke' stopped letting 'the Duchess' touch their money after he caught her naked in their bed with the pool boy. No, that isn't right. It was the maid."

April nearly choked on her champagne. She glanced around. The conversation had moved on, and no one else seemed to have heard Camilla's comment.

"So, you work at the library?" Camilla asked.

"I run it, actually," April replied. "I'm the director."

"And that's how you and Vicki met?"

April glanced at Vicki, who was deep in conversation with Senator Williams. "We're not... We just happened to run into each other tonight," April said for the second time that hour.

"Right."

"Really, I'm supposed to be working right now," she said, looking guiltily at her almost empty glass of champagne. "Vicki just wanted to show me around." April still wasn't sure what Vicki was showing her. After Vicki's comments earlier, she was starting to wonder if this was all a big joke.

"You're not missing out on much," Camilla said. "I'd rather be home in a nice relaxing bath, but, social obligations and all."

April smiled. She was beginning to like this woman.

"Your little pitch was the most interesting thing I've heard all night," Camilla said.

"It wasn't meant to be a pitch. I care a lot about the library, that's all."

"I can tell. Your passion will take you far in life. I'll speak with Vicki about helping out the library." Camilla finished off the last of her drink. "Now, if you'll excuse me, I'm going to go find some more wine. God knows I'll need it to get through the rest of the night." Without another word, Camilla slipped away.

Vicki took the opportunity to pull April to the side. But April was tired of being dragged around. And she hadn't forgotten about Vicki's comments about the library earlier.

She put her hands on her hips. "What the hell was that, Victoria?"

CHAPTER SEVENTEEN

"Let me explain," Vicki said.

"What is there to explain?" April threw her hands up. "You just disparaged West Heights and the people who live there to your rich friends!"

"I had to get you fired up about the library somehow."

"What the hell are you talking about?"

Vicki held her palms out in front of her. "Hear me out."

"Fine," April said. "Talk."

"You were just speaking with Camilla, right?" Vicki said. "Not only is she one of my good friends, but she comes from a very wealthy, influential family. The Robinson's are old money. They have fingers in every pot. Politics, banking, real estate. I wouldn't be surprised if tonight's big anonymous donation came from Camilla."

"What's your point?" April asked.

"This is why I asked you to come mingle. I wanted you to talk to all these people." Vicki gestured around the hall. "This room is filled with the most important people in the city. These are the people who hold all the power. They're who you need to lobby if you want to protect West Heights. We both know that all the changes happening in the city are inevitable. But if you work with those in power instead of against them, you can have a say in how those changes are implemented. Direct where the money goes, make sure that there are policies in place to protect the vulnerable, and so on."

"How am I supposed to do that?" April asked. "I run a library. I don't have all these connections like you do."

"You don't need to," Vicki replied. "At least, not yet. Ever since that town hall meeting, I've been thinking about how good you'd be at politics."

"Me? Politics?"

Vicki nodded. "If you want to make a difference, that's how you can do it. You have a talent for it. You took on Oasis and made us listen to you. You even convinced 'the Duchess' that libraries are a good thing. Obviously, running for office takes time, so it won't help the library's current situation."

"Running for office?" April shook her head. "Why do you of all people want me to do something like this?"

"Because I believe you could do some real good. I'm not the evil villain you think I am. I care about the city too. And West Heights."

"Considering your comments earlier, I find that hard to believe."

"Like I said, I had to get you fired up." Vicki smiled. "You're much more persuasive that way."

"You tricked me," April said.

"It worked, didn't it? I was trying to prove my point."

Vicki shot April a smoldering look. "And you should know, I find that fire of yours sexy as hell."

April folded her arms on her chest. "You think you can charm me into forgetting what you just did?"

"I'm being honest."

"You're unbelievable."

But as April stared back at Vicki, at her mesmerizing eyes and her charming smile, she realized she couldn't stay mad at Vicki for long. And Vicki looked so captivating in that suit. April allowed her eyes to wander down Vicki's body, then back up again…

April frowned. "Vicki?"

Vicki's gaze had shifted to something behind April, her face set like stone and eyes filled with fury. April turned to see an older couple, a man and a woman with striking blonde hair. The man was glaring at Vicki with the exact same expression as Vicki.

"Victoria," he said.

Vicki's narrowed her eyes. "Dad. Mom."

These are Vicki's parents? The very same parents who had all but disowned her years ago? No wonder Vicki looked so angry.

"What are you doing here?" Vicki asked. "You never come to these things."

"Your mother wanted to attend," her father replied curtly.

For a moment no one spoke. April glanced at Vicki's mother. Her face was vacant, like she was pretending Vicki wasn't even there.

Vicki's father looked his daughter up and down. "Still pretending to be a man? I see you haven't changed."

"No, I haven't changed," Vicki said, her voice filled with venom. "And I'm never going to."

"Of course you're not. You just can't help but do everything you can to humiliate us."

April gaped at him. How could anyone treat their own child with such disdain?

"I see *you* haven't changed either," Vicki said. "You still believe the world revolves around you. How arrogant do you have to be to think that I am who I am just to spite you?"

"Why else would you persist in behaving this way?" her father asked. "It's like everything you do is some selfish ploy to shame the family. Dressing like this. Taking a job with those Oasis bastards. Parading around the city with gold-digging sluts on your arm." He gestured toward April.

Vicki seethed. "Say what you want about me, but don't you dare speak about April that way."

"Why not? Whoever this woman is, she's clearly only after you for your money. Why else would she be with someone like you?" He jabbed his finger in Vicki's direction. "You're a disgrace to the Blake family name."

April's hands curled into fists. She had heard enough. "How can you say that?" she said.

Vicki's father looked at April like he'd just been addressed by the wall. "What did you say?"

"How can you say these things about Vicki? Anyone else would be so proud to have a daughter like her! Look at how successful she's become. She's smart, and hardworking, and thoughtful, and brilliant. I don't know how she turned out this way when she had parents like you!" Blood rushed in April's ears. "It's you who should be ashamed."

Vicki's father's face turned crimson. "I'm not going to stand here and be insulted by some lesbian tart."

"Then walk away," Vicki said.

Her father scoffed. "You don't get to tell me what to do."

"Do you really want me to make a scene in front of all these people?" Vicki asked coldly. "I know how much you care about your reputation. I'm not beneath smearing it even more."

Her father glanced around.

"I'll say it again. Walk away and don't come back. Don't ever speak to me again."

Vicki's father scowled. "Don't come crying to us when you end up in trouble."

"It's been ten years," Vicki said. "Ten years since you cut me out of your lives. And I've been doing just fine. I don't need you. I never have."

Vicki's father opened his mouth to retort, then shut it again. He gave Vicki one last glare then took his wife's arm. "Let's go."

Vicki watched them walk away, her body wound tight as a spring.

"Vicki?" April asked. "Are you okay?"

Vicki snapped out of her trance. "I'm fine. Those two know exactly how to get under my skin, that's all." Her brows furrowed. "Are you all right? I can't believe he said those things about you."

"I'm fine." April's heart had finally slowed down to normal. "It helps that I had you to defend my honor. It was kind of sweet."

"Well, you did the same for me." Vicki smiled, her

relaxed demeanor returning. "I had no idea you thought so highly of me."

April flushed. "Don't let it go to your head." She readjusted her mask and glanced around the hall. "I should go check on things."

"All right," Vicki said. "Before you go, I want you to look me in the eyes and admit something."

April's breath caught in her throat. "Admit what?"

"That you enjoyed this."

"You mean cozying up to your snobby friends, then getting in a yelling match with your homophobic father?" April asked.

"Not that part. The rest of it. Drinking champagne, wandering around in this beautiful ballroom together. You had fun, didn't you?"

April looked up at Vicki. Her eyes sparkled under the glittering lights, and her cheeks were faintly flushed with pink. In the tightly packed crowd, the two of them were forced to stand close together, and April could feel the warmth radiating from Vicki's skin.

"Yes," she said. "I enjoyed this."

"See? What did I tell you?"

Vicki reached out and placed a hand on April's arm. Before April knew what she was doing, her hands were on Vicki's shoulders. Then Vicki's hands were at April's waist and their bodies were only inches apart.

April let out a breath. This was stupid. Reckless. The two of them should not be seen together like this. But everyone else was so wrapped up in their own worlds that she and Vicki might as well have been invisible.

And April wanted to pretend.

She slid her hands up and wrapped her arms around Vicki's neck, drawing her down close.

At once, Vicki's lips were on April's, and her hands were at April's hips, holding her so tightly that she wondered how either of them could breathe. April closed her eyes and let her world shrink down until it was just her, and Vicki, alone in the ballroom, melding into each other's skin. April's body begged for so much more than just a kiss.

But she was supposed to be working. And she'd been off with Vicki for much too long.

April broke away. "I really have to go."

"Okay, Cinderella," Vicki said.

April drew back, her hands still clasping Vicki's, not wanting to let go.

"April?"

"Yes?"

"I enjoyed this, too," she said.

Smiling, April released Vicki's hands and walked away.

As she wandered through the crowd, she brought her fingers up to her lips, touching them where Vicki's lips had just been.

CHAPTER EIGHTEEN

*T*he following Tuesday afternoon, April was sitting alone in her office, lost in her head. The library campaign was starting to slow down now, but donations were still trickling in. Between that, and Oasis' willingness to help the library, April was hopeful that everything could actually work out.

Well, everything with the library at least. April was even more confused than ever about herself and Vicki. The constant push and pull between them left her disoriented. That intense kiss they'd shared at the masquerade ball only made things worse. April kept reliving it over and over in her head in an attempt to understand it.

Or maybe she just wanted to experience it again.

April had also been mulling over what Vicki said to her at the ball. Working with those in power, not against them. Doing something bigger. She had never even considered politics before, but she was starting to come around to the idea.

Her thoughts were interrupted when Lexi marched into their office, an inscrutable expression on her face.

She thrust her phone toward April. "Is that you?"

April stared at the photo on the screen. It was from the masquerade ball. The photo was of a group of ladies posing for the camera.

And behind them were April and Vicki, arms around each other, lips locked.

April cursed.

"That's you, isn't it?" Lexi said. "You and Vicki Blake?"

"Y-Yes," April said. This wasn't good. At the very least, April and Vicki were just two of several people in the background of the photo, just faces in a crowd. And they were wearing masks.

But it hadn't been enough to fool Lexi. "I can't believe it," she said.

"Look, Lex, it's complicated-"

"How could it possibly be complicated? Were you drunk? Was it just a momentary lapse?"

"It was more like a series of momentary lapses." April paused. It was time to come clean. "Remember that night we went to The Sapphire Room, and I met someone?"

"Wait, that was her? Vicki Blake?"

April nodded.

Lexi looked like April had slapped her. "You kept that from me all this time?"

"I didn't mean to. I didn't know who she was until that town hall meeting, and then I was embarrassed, and angry, and then I was just in denial about everything." April knew how feeble her excuses sounded.

"That's why you were defending her the other day. Have the two of you been fucking this whole time?"

"It's not like that," April said. "Well, it kind of is. At least, it started off that way. But I think… I'm really starting to care about her, Lexi."

Lexi's expression softened. "Seriously?"

"I don't know." April groaned. "I have so many feelings about her, and some of them are good, and some of them are bad, and I'm so confused."

"Wow." Lexi pulled her chair over to April's desk and sat down next to her. "I didn't think that the two of you were actually serious."

"We're not. I mean, we couldn't possibly be with everything that's going on."

Lexi was silent for a moment. "You could have told me, April."

"How could I?" April asked. "You're always going on about how much of a bad person she is."

"I guess you're right. That would have made it hard, huh?"

April studied her friend. Lexi had a guilty expression on her face. "What is it?" April asked.

Lexi sighed. "You were right, the other day. My grudge against Vicki is kind of personal."

"What do you mean? Did she steal some girl from you?"

Lexi shook her head.

"What, then? Did she try to hit on you?" April asked. "Wait, did something happen between the two of you?"

Lexi shrugged. "Kind of? I mean, we didn't actually sleep together. We almost did."

April felt a sinking feeling in the pit of her stomach. "I didn't know. Vicki never said anything." Vicki had never indicated that she'd met Lexi before, let alone anything more.

"I didn't say anything to you about it either. And I didn't exactly want to share the fact that I'd gotten played by a woman, let alone the woman who is about to bulldoze the library."

"What happened?"

"It was a long time ago," Lexi said. "Back when I was barely old enough to get into a bar. I used to go to Sapphire every weekend, trying to flirt with women and failing more often than not." Lexi smiled. "Believe it or not, I wasn't always this suave. Anyway, Vicki would come to Sapphire all the time too, and she'd have women wrapped around her finger with only a few words."

Yep. That sounded like Vicki.

"I was so jealous of how easy it was for her. Then one night, she came to talk to me, and I was flattered by her attention. I should have known better, but the things she said made me think she was actually interested in me, and not just trying to get into my pants. So, when she asked me if I wanted to go back to her place, I said yes.

"When we got back to her apartment, things got all hot and heavy, then-" Lexi paused. "I don't know what happened exactly. We were both a little drunk. But one minute we were making out on her bed, and the next, Vicki shoved my shirt into my arms, called me a cab, and booted me out the door with zero explanation. I guess she changed her mind? I was pretty upset about it at the time. I'm not sure if I was upset at her for blowing me off, or at myself for falling for her act in the first place. To top it off, I saw her back at Sapphire the next weekend, doing the same thing as always."

"Wow. I'm sorry, Lex," April said.

"Don't be," Lexi replied. "It was years ago. It wasn't that big a deal at the time either. I mean, I was back at Sapphire doing my thing the next week too. I guess I still resent her though." Lexi flicked one of her dark curls out of her eyes. "I don't know, maybe it's justified. Plenty of women out there have been screwed around by Vicki Blake. Word gets around, you know how it is."

April said nothing, unsure of whether she even wanted to defend Vicki.

"Look," Lexi said. "We're all adults here. I'm not going to tell you that you can't date someone because of one night when we almost slept together years ago. I just don't want you to get hurt, that's all."

"I won't," April said. "I'm being careful about this." That was a lie.

"Okay. Sorry I've been such a bitch about her."

"It's all right. Sorry I kept this all from you. Are we okay?"

Lexi nodded. "We are."

Relief washed over April. She couldn't bear the thought of being on bad terms with Lexi. But with that problem resolved, she still had a bigger one.

"Where did you find that photo of Vicki and me?" April asked.

"The photos from the ball are up on the city's website. They have a society pages section. I was checking them out because I wanted to see the fruit of all my hard work. I have to admit, those ice sculptures looked pretty good." Lexi noticed April's frown. "Oh, you're worried people will see the photo?"

"Yeah. I mean, I've somehow become some sort of crusader for West Heights. And Vicki is high up in Oasis's hierarchy. I can't imagine it'll look good for either of us to be caught sleeping with the enemy, so to speak."

"Don't worry," Lexi said. "No one looks at the city's website. And the only reason I spotted you in that picture is because I recognized that red dress of yours. I was there when you bought it for Caroline's wedding last year. With the masks on, no one is going to recognize you."

That did little to reassure April.

"If you're really worried, you can try to get the photo taken down, but that might draw more attention to it. People love to gossip after all. Do you really want Anne down at City Hall wondering why we're so eager to have the photo taken down?"

"That's a good point," April said.

She would have to work out some way to deal with the photo. And she should probably warn Vicki. April asked Lexi for a link to the photo, and she sent it to Vicki along with a quick message. A few minutes later, she received a reply.

Thanks for the warning.

Another message soon followed.

Can you come to my apartment after work so we can talk about this?

Sure, April replied. Two heads were better than one, after all.

Still, the photo wasn't what was on April's mind when she returned to her work. April had definitely mentioned to

Vicki that she and Lexi were friends. Close friends. And she'd had plenty of opportunities to tell April that something had happened between them.

But Vicki had never said a word to her about it.

———

A few hours later, April stepped through the door of Vicki's apartment. Vicki was dressed casually in a loose white shirt and jeans. Her feet were bare, and her hair was slightly ruffled, but she still managed to look incredibly sexy.

Vicki told April to sit down while she cleared her laptop and a stack of documents from the coffee table.

"Working late?" April asked.

"I was," Vicki replied. "But I'm glad you're here. I can't stand to look at another spreadsheet. Do you want a drink? Coffee? Something stronger?"

"Something stronger is about my speed right now," April said.

"Lucky for you, I have a well-stocked bar. Have a seat."

April sat down while Vicki disappeared into the kitchen. Something black and furry leaped onto the table beside her. Sebastian. He sat there, unmoving, watching her with his usual disdainful expression. April was about to ask him what she'd ever done to deserve his scorn when Vicki returned with two mojitos. She handed one to April and sat down next to her, stretching out her long limbs.

"Looks like we were caught in the act," Vicki said.

"Yeah," April said. "What do we do? Try to get it taken down? Ignore it, and cross our fingers that no one notices it? I mean, it looks pretty bad. Could it get you in trouble with Oasis?"

"I'm not too worried. Men in positions like mine get caught doing far more scandalous things. At the work Christmas party last year, our VP of finance got caught with his hand up his secretary's skirt, and no one batted an eyelid. Except for his wife."

April raised an eyebrow.

"Not that this is the same thing, of course," Vicki said quickly. "You're right, it doesn't look good. But it'll be okay. We'll figure out how to handle it. At the very least, we're barely recognizable unless you look closely."

That was exactly what Lexi had said. *Lexi*. April had to ask Vicki about Lexi, but she wasn't sure if there was an answer Vicki could give her that would satisfy her.

"I looked through the photos already, and I didn't even notice," Vicki said. "You have a better eye than I do."

"It wasn't me who spotted us. It was Lexi." April examined Vicki's face for any sign of recognition.

"We're lucky she found it, then," Vicki said.

"You know Lexi, don't you? My friend who works at the library with me."

"She's the event coordinator, right? She was at the meetings we had at the library."

"You've met before that," April said.

"I have?" Vicki asked. "She did seem familiar."

April frowned. Suddenly, it hit her. Vicki hadn't deliberately kept this from April. "You don't remember her, do you?"

Vicki's forehead creased. "What's this about? You're going to have to help me out here."

April crossed her arms. "You picked Lexi up at Sapphire once."

Realization dawned on Vicki's face. "You're right."

"You actually forgot, didn't you?" April shook her head. "Unbelievable."

"I was drunk," Vicki protested. "And we didn't sleep together. Besides, it was years ago. It would have been back when I…"

"When what?"

"When I was going through some things. I was young, and I went off the rails. It's a period of my life that I prefer to forget."

"That's supposed to justify it?" April wasn't sure exactly what 'it' was. The way Vicki had toyed with Lexi? The fact that Vicki had forgotten about ever taking her home? Everything that said about Vicki? It was all tangled up in one big knot in April's head.

"No, of course not," Vicki said. "I take full responsibility for the way I behaved. I treated Lexi badly, and I'm sorry."

This wasn't the reaction April was expecting. "Aren't you going to try to explain yourself?"

"I'm not going to make excuses for my behavior."

"I don't want excuses. I want to know why." April's voice quavered. "And I want to know that you're not that person anymore."

"That person?" Vicki said. "You mean that spoiled, rich womanizer who leads women on and only cares about herself?"

"I didn't say that."

"I'm aware of what people say about me. The truth is, I earned that reputation. As for whether I'm still that person?

I'd like to think I'm not." Vicki folded her hands in her lap. "Look, to start off with, I want you to know that I didn't keep this from you on purpose. I would never keep something from you that I thought would hurt you."

April felt a twinge in her chest.

"As for why I behaved the way I did that night and so many other nights? It's complicated." Vicki stared intently at her barely touched drink. "You've seen firsthand what my parents are like. Things were tough for me growing up. As an outsider in my own family, I lived a lonely life. It left me with a lot of scars. As an adult, I struggled to form meaningful relationships, so instead, I formed superficial ones. And I'm not proud to say it, but I embraced the advantages my privilege gave me. I played the role of the rich playgirl, drinking, flirting, and throwing around money to win women over. It was an easy way for me to feel a connection with someone, even if it wasn't real."

A heavy ache filled April's stomach. She knew what it was like to be an outsider, to feel that desperate loneliness.

"That night with Lexi was around the time my parents cut me out of their lives. I was in a bad place, so I spent my days and nights indulging in all my favorite vices. I was careless about it, too. And Lexi was one of the victims of my callousness.

"I regret the way I behaved back then," Vicki said. "I'm not proud of the person I was. And I'm sorry for the way I treated your friend." Vicki placed her hand on April's. "I'm not that person anymore. It's taken a long time, but I've changed, and grown, and I'm trying to be better."

April searched Vicki's face, unsure whether she was looking for a reason to believe Vicki, or a reason not to believe her. The truth was, April had been looking for reasons not to trust her since day one, reasons to deny her feelings for Vicki.

But April couldn't ignore them any longer.

"I can't hold your past against you," April finally said. "And you've shed your womanizing ways?"

"Of course," Vicki replied. "You're the only woman I've been with in god knows how long. It took me a while, but I realized how hollow that life was. I kept going to my old haunts, but I always went home alone. The night I met you, I wasn't lying when I said I was hoping someone exceptional would walk through the door. And you did." Vicki smiled. "Of course, as soon as I started talking to you, I went into player mode out of habit. But I never meant for you to be a one-night stand."

"Really?" April asked. "Because I remember you being very eager to get me out of my dress."

"What, a woman can't want both sex *and* a relationship?"

April stared at her. "You wanted a relationship?"

"Well, I wasn't going to ask you to move in after one night," Vicki said. "But I wanted to get to know you and see where things could go between us. And then the town hall meeting happened."

April was silent. There was a question that had been lingering at the back of her mind for a while now.

"Have you ever wondered what would have happened if it wasn't for, well, everything?" April asked. "Do you think that if the circumstances were different, there could have been something between us?"

"I'd like to think so," Vicki said. "Who knows, maybe

once everything with the library is resolved, we can start over, give a real relationship a try?"

A real relationship. It seemed like such a distant possibility. But right now, April wanted nothing more. "I would like that." April smiled. "That is, as long as that relationship isn't-" What was the word Vicki always used? "—*vanilla.*"

A spark lit up behind Vicki's eyes. "Are you saying you still want to be my submissive?"

"I'm saying, I want you to make good on your promise to give me a taste of all those toys in your closet."

"Oh, April. When are you going to learn? It's not about the toys and tools." Vicki pushed April down onto the couch and leaned over her, speaking into April's ear. "It's about power."

CHAPTER NINETEEN

*B*efore April knew what was happening, Vicki was on top of her, and Vicki's hands were at her wrists, pinning them to the arm of the couch above April's head. April wriggled underneath her, trying to break free, but Vicki had her trapped with what seemed like no effort at all.

April's whole body lit up. "Kiss me," she said breathlessly.

Instead, Vicki adjusted her grip on April's wrists so that she was holding them with one hand. She dragged her other hand along April's cheek and stared down at her, her jade eyes filled with fire. She dipped down low to draw her lips across the bow of April's neck and down to her chest, sucking and nibbling the swell of her breast that peeked out the top of her dress. Her hand traveled down to grab April's ass cheek.

April groaned. "Kiss me?"

Vicki glided her hand along the back of April's thigh, hoisting April's leg up to wrap around her waist. She shifted her body, grinding her hips between April's thighs, kissing her everywhere but her lips. The seam of Vicki's jeans rubbed against April through her dress, sending jolts deep into her core. She arched her chest up, trying in vain to press her body against Vicki's.

She closed her eyes and spoke the only words that could sway Vicki. "Please," April said. "Kiss me, *please*."

Finally, Vicki grabbed April's chin and pressed her lips on April's. At once, April came apart. She melted into Vicki's body, her mind emptying. Her need for the other woman was so strong that she felt like she was going to burst. Vicki's suffocating kisses told April that Vicki felt the same.

She released April's hands and tore April's dress over her head. April grasped a fistful of Vicki's shirt, so she could pull Vicki down to her.

But Vicki pushed April's wrist down to the couch. "Don't move." Without another word, she got up and disappeared into her bedroom.

April groaned. Just when things were heating up, Vicki left her throbbing on the couch. Whatever Vicki was getting from her bedroom better be worth it. April's frustration only intensified when she thought about all the toys in Vicki's closet and the chest at the end of her bed.

When Vicki finally emerged, it was immediately clear to April what she had been doing in her room. She had taken off her jeans, and her long shirt was unbuttoned, with nothing underneath. Belted around her hips was a dark red strap-on.

Suddenly, there was a hollowness inside April that only Vicki could satisfy.

Vicki strode up to the couch. "This is what I was looking

for in my chest that night I picked you up at the bar," she said. "Before you spoiled everything by being nosy."

April gave her a cheeky smile. "Aren't you glad that I did?"

Vicki's response was to fall on top of April again, assailing her with ravenous lips and hands. Somehow, Vicki managed to tear off April's bra and panties, tossing them across the room. Once again, April found herself helplessly trapped by Vicki's embrace.

April clung to her, craving the feel of Vicki's skin against hers. Vicki was just as hungry as April. She groped at April's curves, clawed at her skin, frantically working her way over April's entire body. April trembled. Vicki's body against hers, Vicki's scent, the taste of her skin, the hard strap-on pressing against her—it all threatened to overwhelm her. April could feel them being swept away in a firestorm of lust.

Vicki pulled back. "Wait."

"Is something wrong?" April asked. Vicki's expression was unreadable.

"No, of course not." Vicki gazed back down at April. "Everything is perfect. Which is why I want to take my time. I want to savor every moment. I don't want this to end," she said softly.

April's heart began to thump. "Okay."

Vicki kissed April again, softly this time. Tentatively, April reached up to push Vicki's shirt from her shoulders and drew Vicki to her. As the kiss stretched out, April allowed her fingertips to explore every part of Vicki's body. Her narrow shoulders. Her slender thighs. Her soft ass.

Vicki's hands mirrored April's, her hands roaming over

April's skin. April could feel Vicki's restraint in every kiss and every touch. April yearned to tell Vicki to stop holding back, to devour her like she always did. But then everything would be over too quickly. April didn't want this to end either.

April kissed a line down Vicki's breasts and circled her nipple with her tongue. She brought a hand up to the other nipple, brushing her fingertips over the pebbled bud. A fevered murmur rose from Vicki's chest, her whole body shuddering. April reveled in Vicki's unbridled reactions. Who knew that the tough, dominant woman was so sensitive and responsive?

Vicki's hand found its way between April's legs. She slipped a finger inside, teasing April with a shadow of what was to come. The heel of her palm pressed against April's clit. April pushed against her, desperate and aching.

Just when April couldn't take it any longer, Vicki grabbed the strap-on, drawing it down April's slit, and entered her.

April exhaled sharply. God, Vicki felt so good inside. Vicki began to pump in and out, slowly, making every stroke count. April clutched onto her, rising up to meet her over and over.

This wasn't the Vicki of every other night, the hurricane of a woman fueled only by passion. She was just as possessive, and just as insatiable. But she was soft, and tender, and measured. With every movement, Vicki let out a gasp, a faint echo of April's own unrestrained cries. When April looked into Vicki's green eyes, April could see her own boundless desire reflected in them.

April closed her eyes. Vicki was right. It wasn't about all

the toys, and the tools, and the kink. It wasn't even the power games that made April submit to Vicki every single time.

It was her. It had always been her.

"Victoria," April said. "I'm yours."

At once, Vicki shifted her hips, delving into April with urgent thrusts. April cried out as her pleasure rose to a crescendo and flooded her whole being. At the same time, Vicki shivered in April's arms, her climax mirroring April's.

***

Afterward, they ended up in Vicki's bed. April lay nestled against Vicki's shoulder, the blonde woman's arm slung around her. Did Vicki's hair always smell this heavenly?

"You know," Vicki said. "You never finished telling me why the library is so important to you."

"It's a little childish," April said.

"So what if it's childish? Whatever your reasons, they're important to you, and that means something."

"You're right." April drew back, laying her head on the pillow next to Vicki's. "The library was my refuge during a difficult time in my life. That was when I was a teenager. But even now, it holds an important place in my heart."

"It's your sanctuary," Vicki said.

"Yes." April looked at her in surprise. She hadn't expected Vicki to remember that. "You see, when I was in high school, I got bullied a lot."

"Really? You're the fiercest person I've ever met. I can't imagine anyone picking on you."

"I was different back then. Besides, bullying doesn't

happen because of the victim's personality. Bullies target people for all kinds of reasons. In my case, I was just unlucky. There was this clique of mean girls everyone was afraid of. One day, out of nowhere, they set their sights on me. I was a quiet, nerdy kid who liked books and kept to myself. I was an easy target for them because they knew no one would stand up for me. So they picked on me relentlessly."

"That must have been difficult," Vicki said.

"It was, especially at first. As time went on, I went to the library more and more after school. I used books as an escape, to pretend I was someone else, somewhere else. I made friends at the library, kids from other schools who were outsiders like me. And I met Eliza. She was the librarian back then, and only ten years older than me. She took me under her wing, gave me advice, and she didn't treat me like my problems weren't real because I was just a kid. As I got older, we became friends. She gave me my first job as a page at the library when I was still in school and offered me another job when I returned from college. She promoted me to director when she left earlier in the year."

"She's a smart woman," Vicki said.

April smiled. "Anyway, by the time I was a junior, the bullies got bored with me and moved on to other targets. I'm ashamed to admit I was happy about that. I didn't care that they were hurting others as long as it wasn't me. It was selfish."

"That's not selfish," Vicki said. "That's just self-preservation."

"Well, I didn't feel good about it. So, after high school, I told myself that I would never stand by and let anything like that happen again, to myself or anyone else. That I wouldn't let bullies win, and I'd stand up for the people around me."

"And so, you became April, defender of the downtrodden. It all makes sense now."

April shrugged. "I guess so. That's why the library is so important to me. It's been mine for so long. That's why I can't bear the thought of it being destroyed."

"I understand," Vicki said. "And I mean it when I say that I'm committed to helping you find a way to save it. We can't save Oakmont Street, but I'll do my best to make sure the library survives."

"Thanks, Vicki." April let out a contented sigh. "You know, all this time we've spent together has made me realize something. That person I became after high school—someone who always stands up, who fights back—it's made me forget how to let my guard down."

"That's never easy for anyone," Vicki said.

"Well, for me it's been toxic. It's probably why my relationships always end up falling apart. But when you came along, you were offering me exactly what I wanted. I wanted to be vulnerable but didn't know how to let myself. You were right all along. And your strength made me feel like it was safe for me to do that with you. Does that make sense?"

"It does," Vicki replied.

"I'm glad you gave me a chance to try to be your submissive," April said. "I'm not a very good one."

"That's not true. There's no right or wrong way to be a submissive. There are lots of submissives like you, who like to push back, who need to test their dominants to feel at ease." Vicki propped herself up and looked down at April.

"Of course, their dominants usually push back even harder, whereas I've been letting you off easy."

"Letting me off easy?" April scoffed. "Last time I was here, you made me wait for you, blindfolded, for god knows how long. And then you tied me to the chair! How is that letting me off easy?"

"Oh April, you have no idea." Vicki chuckled softly. "If anyone knew about all the things I let you get away with, they'd take away my Domme card."

April frowned. "Do you really have a card?"

"Come here." Vicki wrapped her arms around April. "I'm glad I took a chance with you too. It feels good, to be challenged. All this time, I've been wandering through life, just going through the motions. BDSM was just a way for me to feel intimacy without having to get too close to anyone. Then you came along and actually made me feel something real. You made me want to let go of my grip on control and give in to passion. It's been so long since I've done that. I was beginning to forget what it feels like."

"I guess we both needed to step out of our comfort zones a little." April ran her fingers through Vicki's soft, weightless hair. "Does this mean you want me to push your boundaries even more?"

Vicki gave her a stern look. "Don't even think about it."

April rested her head on Vicki's chest. She couldn't help but wonder how she got here. Most of the upheaval and chaos in April's life right now was because of Vicki. But as she lay there next to Vicki, she began to wonder if maybe her sanctuary could be a person instead of a place.

"April," Vicki said. "Stay the night."

Vicki's voice had that compelling quality to it, the one

that made it impossible for April to say no to her. And April didn't want to say no.

"Okay," April said. "I'll stay."

Vicki drew her in for a kiss. April closed her eyes, wishing that she'd never have to pull away.

But at the back of her mind, she was aware that everything was still up in the air. The library. The photo of them at the ball.

This wasn't pretend anymore. The two of them couldn't hide behind passion and power games any longer. Their two worlds were colliding.

April hoped they could survive the impact.

CHAPTER TWENTY

*A*pril wrapped another plate in newspaper and added it to the box. It was Friday evening, and she was helping Eliza pack. Eliza wasn't leaving for another week, but she had an entire house to box up.

April sighed. Eliza leaving was just one of her myriad worries.

"That's it," Eliza said. "I'm sick of all your sighing. Sit down. What's wrong?"

April sat down on the couch next to her. "I have a lot on my mind at the moment, that's all."

"Like what?" Eliza asked.

"Well, there's everything with the library."

"I thought you were making progress?"

"We are," April replied. "Now that that the development project is on hold, we have enough time to look into long-term funding options."

"That all sounds promising," Eliza said. "So what's really the matter?"

"It's complicated."

"Try me."

"There's someone I have feelings for," April said. "Serious feelings. I don't think I've ever felt this way about anyone." She fidgeted with her fingers in her lap. "I think I'm falling in love with her."

Eliza smiled. "And what's the problem?"

"She's someone I shouldn't have feelings for. Someone I shouldn't be with."

"Why not?"

"Because she's Vicki Blake."

"Oh." Eliza paused. "Does she feel the same way?"

"I don't know," April said. "We've talked about giving a relationship a try once things with the library are sorted out. But that could take months. With everything else that's going on, it just seems impossible that we could ever actually be together."

"Impossible? I'm sure it'll be hard, but it's far from impossible," Eliza said. "The two of you will be able to work things out. Just hang in there and be patient."

"I hope you're right."

"I am." Eliza gave April a reassuring pat on the arm. "Now, I can handle the rest of this. Why don't you go home?"

"Are you sure? I don't mind helping out some more."

"It's okay. It's Friday night. You should go home and put your feet up."

"That does sound nice." With the charity ball last weekend, it had been a while since she'd had any downtime.

April said goodbye to Eliza and headed toward her apartment. Her mind drifted to Vicki. April wondered what it would be like to spend a quiet Friday night in with her, like a normal couple, without all the craziness that came with their present relationship. Of course, even if they were a normal couple, their relationship would probably still be crazy. Two headstrong women like them? Where there were sparks, there was bound to be fire. But April liked fire.

April wasn't even halfway home before her phone rang. It was Lexi.

"April, hi," she said. "How are you?"

"I'm fine," April replied. It was a strange question for Lexi to ask, considering they'd seen each other at work a few hours ago.

"Are you at home right now?"

"I'm on my way back from Eliza's, I'll be home soon. Why?" Something in Lexi's voice had her worried.

"I'm coming over, I'll explain when I get there."

"Don't you have a date?" April was sure that Lexi had mentioned she had plans tonight.

"I did. It's fine."

"Lexi, what's going on?"

"It's nothing. Look, I'll be there in half an hour, okay?" Lexi hung up.

April stared at her phone, frowning. She hoped that Lexi was okay.

She reached her apartment a few minutes later. She had some time to kill before Lexi arrived, so she sat down with her laptop and checked her social media feed. Although most of the discussion surrounding the library had died down, there was some local chatter about the Oakmont Street project in general, as well as other developments going on around West Heights. As April scrolled through her feed idly, a post caught her eye.

Her stomach dropped. It was the photo from the ball, with April and Vicki in the background. And someone had drawn a big red circle around them.

Shit. April looked at the name of the person who posted the photo. It was a woman who April didn't know, but they had a handful of mutual friends. April scanned the comments underneath the photo.

That's Victoria Blake. She's one of the top brass at Oasis. What's April doing with her?

What a liar. Acting like she cares about West Heights while she's in league with the developers.

She's a lesbian? I always knew there was something weird about her in high school.

What a fucking hypocrite.

April felt a clenching in her chest. The rest of the comments were more of the same. She didn't even know who half the people commenting were. But that didn't make their words hurt any less. April had been called names before. Ganged up on. Bullied. And all those memories were flooding back.

April took a few deep breaths. Everything was fine. She was fine. And she needed to tell Vicki about this. She picked up the phone and dialed Vicki's number. But the phone kept ringing and ringing until it went to voicemail. She tried again. The same thing happened.

April sent Vicki a message.

I need to talk to you. Call me.

April glanced at her laptop screen.

I can't believe I donated to her stupid fundraiser. This is fraud!

Now we know whose side she's really on.

April shut her laptop. She couldn't look at it anymore. Moments later, she received a reply from Vicki.

Can't talk. Busy with work.

April cursed. *It's important. Can you call me when you get a minute?*

Vicki's response was a single word. *Later.*

April set her phone down, her stomach roiling with unease. Sure, she'd called Vicki to warn her that the photo was out. But more than anything, April just wanted to talk to her. Of course, it was silly to expect Vicki to drop everything for her.

For the next half hour, April paced and fretted. When she finally managed to calm herself down, there was a knock on her door. For a moment, she wondered if it was Vicki. Then she realized how unlikely that was. Vicki hadn't even called her back.

April opened the door to find Lexi standing out in the hall. In her flustered state, April had forgotten that Lexi was coming over.

"Shit," Lexi said. "You saw the photo, didn't you?"

April nodded.

"How are you holding up?"

"I've been better," April said. "Come on in."

April sat back down on the couch, her legs tucked under her, as Lexi made them tea. Eliza's tea habit had spread to everyone who worked at the library.

Lexi returned to the living room carrying two mugs. "Here." She handed one to April and sat down next to her. "Sorry for the weird phone call. I was hoping you hadn't seen the post yet."

April wrapped her hands around the warm mug. "When

I thought about the photo getting out, I wasn't expecting it to show up on social media like this," April said. "I don't even know the woman who posted it."

"I do," Lexi said. "She's city hall's resident busybody. Works for the mayor. And we both know that the Mayor isn't too happy that you made her look bad."

"What, so one of her employees decided to make me look bad too? That's so petty." April sighed. "I don't even care that people know about Vicki and me. I just don't understand why everyone is being so mean."

Lexi shrugged. "That's the dark side of social media."

"But these people don't even know me! Some of them have nothing to do with the library or West Heights! Why do they even care?"

"Don't let it get to you. They're just sad little people hiding behind their screens who have nothing better to do than badmouth others online.

"It feels like the whole world is against me," April said softly. "It's like high school all over again."

Lexi held out her arms and pulled April into a hug. "I know it feels that way. But no one who matters has seen this or thinks you're a hypocrite. And we can fix this. I'll help you get the photo and all the comments taken down."

"Thanks, Lex."

"That's what friends are for," Lexi replied. "You know what else will help? Takeout and a bad movie. Why don't you order dinner while I take care of this?"

April gave her a half smile. "Okay."

An hour later, the two of them were watching a fluffy rom-com while stuffing themselves with Chinese food. Lexi was right. It had taken April's mind off everything.

Except for Vicki.

April checked her phone again. Nothing. Was Vicki really still working at nine p.m. on a Friday night? April couldn't help but feel like she was being brushed off. Or maybe she was reading too much into Vicki's terse messages.

"Are you okay?" Lexi asked.

"Yeah," April said. "I'm waiting for Vicki to call me back, that's all."

"Does she know what's going on?"

"I'm not sure. She's pretty busy with work."

Lexi gave April a sympathetic look. "I'm sure she'll call you back when she has time."

"Yeah. You're right." April yawned and stretched out her arms, then realized this was the first time Lexi had said anything remotely supportive about Vicki. "Does this mean that you don't disapprove of Vicki anymore?"

"I've been holding a grudge against her for too long," Lexi said. "And I know that you really care about her. If you say she's changed, I believe you."

April should have been happy that Lexi had finally come around on Vicki. Instead, April was the one filled with doubts about her.

The rest of the night passed quickly. By the time Lexi left, it was late. All April wanted to do was go to sleep and forget about the events of the day. But now that she was alone in her apartment, her worries bubbled to the surface.

As she got into bed, she took one last look at her phone. Still nothing from Vicki. She opened up the last message she had sent. It was now labeled 'seen.' Vicki had seen the message. She just hadn't bothered responding, despite April telling her it was important.

April placed her phone on the nightstand. Now, when she needed Vicki the most, she was nowhere to be found. Maybe Lexi had been right all along. April had fallen for Vicki's sweet, empty words.

April never should have trusted her.

CHAPTER TWENTY-ONE

The weekend passed, and April's doubts about Vicki only grew. She'd sent Vicki a couple more messages, only to receive vague responses about a 'work crisis.' April could have simply sent Vicki a message about the photo, but she was too angry at Vicki for brushing her off.

So April spent most of the weekend with Lexi, trying to keep her mind off everything. Thanks to Lexi, the photo disappeared from social media, along with all the comments. Still, April felt awful about everything.

When she woke up on Monday morning, it was ten a.m. April groaned. She had slept through her alarm. She had never been late for work in her life.

April rolled over to check her phone. Half of her hoped to find that Vicki had finally called her, while the other half was too mad at her to want to speak to her.

But there was nothing from Vicki. Instead, April found dozens of calls and panicked texts from Lexi. She opened up one of the messages.

Where are you? Something is happening at the library. Call me.

April's stomach sank. She dialed Lexi's number.

Lexi was frantic when she picked up. "April? Are you okay? Where are you?"

"I'm fine, I just overslept," April said. "What's going on with the library?"

"There's a guy here saying that we need to shut it down. *Today.*"

April's blood ran cold. This wasn't happening. Vicki had promised. She had said they had time.

"I'm trying to get Vicki or someone from Oasis on the phone, but they're giving me the runaround," Lexi said. "I don't know what else to do."

April pushed her worries about Vicki aside. She had to focus on what was important. She vaulted out of bed and grabbed some clothes. "I'm on my way."

When April arrived at the library, Lexi was standing out front, arguing animatedly with a man in a suit. He was brandishing a sheet of paper like a shield.

"Look, I'm just the messenger," he said. "I don't know anything. You'll have to speak to whoever's running the project."

"I've been trying to get someone on the phone for the last twenty minutes!" Lexi said.

"That's not my problem."

April approached them. "What's going on?"

Lexi gestured toward the man. "Oasis has sent some

lackey over to tell us the library is being shut down and we need to vacate the building next week."

"That can't be right. The development project is on hold. The library is supposed to stay open until we can find another location."

"Like I told her, I don't know anything about the project. I'm just here to deliver this." The man handed April the paper in his hand. "I'm not getting paid enough to deal with this," he muttered.

April skimmed the page. It was an eviction notice. They had seven days to get out of the building. This was even shorter than the three months they'd originally been given.

"This doesn't make any sense," April said.

She looked at the signature at the bottom. It wasn't Vicki's. Where was she in all this? At worst, this was Vicki's doing. At best, she would have known about it. Why hadn't she said anything to April?

Why hadn't she stopped this?

"April, can you call Vicki?" Lexi asked.

April tried to speak, but there was a lump in her throat.

"Oh, thank god." The man was looking toward the street. "Here's Ms. Blake now. You can talk to her about this."

April turned to follow his gaze. Sure enough, Vicki was hurrying over to them. April clenched her fists, anger boiling up inside her.

She marched over to Vicki, meeting her on the sidewalk. "What the hell, Victoria? This man is saying that we have to shut down the library?"

"April," Vicki began. "I can explain-"

"Just tell me it isn't true."

"It is. I'm sorry."

"No." April's voice quavered. "How could you let this happen?"

"The decision went above my head," Vicki said. "A few of Oasis' major projects fell through, so the board decided that they couldn't put the Oakmont Street development on hold any longer."

"The board?" April asked. "So you had nothing to do with it?"

"I was overruled. I tried everything I could to stop this, April. I spent all weekend trying to stop this."

April furrowed her brows. "This was the crisis you were dealing with at work."

Vicki nodded.

"You've known the library was going to be shut down for *three whole days*?" April's voice rose. "Did it ever occur to you to tell me?"

"It did, but-" Vicki brought her hand to her forehead. "Look, I *know* I shouldn't have kept this from you, but I wanted to try to fix it first. I thought that I could salvage one of our other projects, so there wouldn't be any need to rush the Oakmont Street development. I almost pulled it off too, but everything fell apart this morning."

"Is that your excuse for ignoring me all weekend?" April asked.

"It was stupid. But I know how much the library means to you. I knew you'd be devastated if you found out. I didn't want to tell you if I didn't have to. And I knew that if I spoke to you, I'd have to tell you what was going on. I was trying to spare your feelings-"

"*My feelings?* I'm not some delicate fucking girl. I don't need you to protect me. And if you really cared about my feelings, you wouldn't have ignored me like you did. Do you have any idea what I've been going through for the past few days?"

"What do you mean?" Vicki asked.

"You don't even know, do you?" April said. "Someone found the photo of us and posted it on social media, and everyone is calling me a liar, and a hypocrite, and worse for being in bed with you."

A look of horror crossed Vicki's face. "I had no idea. Are you all right?"

"Of course I'm not all right! I needed you. I needed you and you weren't there."

"I'm so sorry," Vicki said.

April crossed her arms. "It doesn't matter. What matters is that I trusted you. You promised me that you wouldn't let the library get shut down."

"I tried to stop this. I got into an argument with the CEO that almost got me fired!"

"Seriously? I'm supposed to care that you almost got fired from your cushy million-dollar job?"

"That's not what I meant." Vicki let out an exasperated groan. "What I'm trying to say is that I did everything in my power to stop this from happening, but it wasn't enough."

"You promised me," April said quietly.

"I'm sorry. Really, I am. And I messed up by keeping this from you. I'll do whatever I can to help."

April shook her head, her eyes clouding with tears. "It's too late, Victoria. You're too late."

April turned and walked back toward the library. Mercifully, Vicki didn't try to follow her. Lexi was waiting by the front door. The man had left.

"What happened?" Lexi asked.

"It's over. The library is shutting down and there's nothing we can do about it."

Lexi cursed quietly. "You and Vicki?"

April shook her head. "You were right about her. You were right about everything. I should never have trusted her."

"I'm sorry." Lexi wrapped her arm around April's shoulders. "For what it's worth, I really hoped I was wrong about her."

"So did I," April said.

CHAPTER TWENTY-TWO

*O*ver the course of the next seven days, April, Lexi and the other staff packed up the library. Everything was going into storage. Although the building would be reduced to rubble in a matter of weeks, the sudden nature of the Oakmont Street building's closure meant that the city hadn't officially shut down the library yet, but it was only a matter of time.

The somber mood in the library weighed heavily on April. It didn't help that everyone who worked there had heard about April and Vicki. Although Lexi had gotten the photo and the nasty comments taken down, word had gotten around. Lexi assured April that none of the staff held it against her. They all knew she had fought harder for the library than anyone else. It did little to make April feel better.

April grabbed a handful of books from the shelf and slipped them into the box at her feet. She looked down the almost empty aisle. Once they were finished with these last few shelves, there would be nothing left.

This was the end of Oakmont Street Library.

"Are you all right?" Lexi asked April.

"Yeah. It's just sad to see all this go."

"You never know," Lexi said. "Oasis might pull through with that old building they originally offered to lease us. It'll be better than nothing."

"I'm not holding my breath," April said.

After giving the library the eviction notice, Oasis had gone back to radio silence. April hadn't heard from Vicki about the library or anything else, but she was too mad to speak to her, anyway. Lexi had taken over trying to get in touch with Oasis, but she'd been informed that Vicki was "no longer working on the Oakmont Street project", and she had a hard time getting through to anyone else.

April wondered why Vicki wasn't working on the project anymore. April hadn't heard from her since the day they had fought outside the library. She shouldn't have been disappointed that Vicki had washed her hands of April and the library. She'd shown her true colors in the end, after all. As far as April was concerned, the two of them were done.

Yet, whenever April thought about her, she felt something pulling in her chest. She'd shown Vicki a side of herself that she had never shown to anyone else. If it wasn't for Vicki, April wouldn't even have known that part of her existed. She would never have come to accept that the April who fought fiercely for those around her could coexist with the April who craved the freedom that came with vulnerability.

It didn't matter. Right from the start, the chances that things could have worked out between them had been slim. It had been foolish of April to think otherwise.

April taped up her box of books and scanned the shelves before her. There wasn't much left to pack up. "Mind if I head off?" she asked Lexi. "I want to go see Eliza. She's leaving in the morning."

"Sure," Lexi said. "Say goodbye to her for me."

"Will you be all right with the rest of this?"

"Yeah, it's not much. Once we're done here, I have to clean out my side of the office, and that's it."

That's it. Goodbye Oakmont Street. "I should get going," April said.

"I'll see you tomorrow morning to hand the place over."

April hesitated. She reached into her pocket and pulled out her set of keys to the building. "Do you think you could handle it by yourself?"

"Sure." Lexi took the keys from her.

April made her way to Eliza's house, watching the neighborhood go by as she walked. Half of the buildings looked unfamiliar. Lexi had been right all that time ago. What happened to the library was inevitable. April had been naive to think she could take on a corporate giant like Oasis.

By the time April made it to Eliza's house, she was a wreck. She tried to keep it together for Eliza's sake, but Eliza could see through her.

She gave April a hug. "Come on in. I'll make tea."

April sat down at Eliza's kitchen table. The house was almost empty, save for some furniture and essentials. Soon, the two of them were drinking tea out of chipped, mismatched mugs and sharing stories about the library.

"Remember that guy who brought back those overdue books from the 80s?" April asked.

Eliza nodded. "He borrowed them when he was a

teenager and forgot about them. They still had the old borrowing cards in the front." She chuckled. "Do you remember when the computer system broke down and we had to use the card catalog for a week?"

"That was a nightmare." April sighed. "I'm really going to miss that place. And I'm going to miss you."

"I'll miss you too."

"I mean it. You've been such a big part of my life for so long, I just can't imagine it without you."

Eliza smiled. "You'll be fine. And you're welcome to come visit any time."

"Thanks, Eliza," April said.

They sipped their tea in comfortable silence. They were already onto their third cup. April was all too aware that this was the last time she'd get to sit at Eliza's kitchen table drinking tea with her.

"Have you spoken to Vicki yet?" Eliza asked.

April stared down into her cup. "No." Eliza had been sympathetic about everything that had happened with Vicki, but April couldn't help but feel like Eliza thought she was being irrational.

"Tell me this," Eliza said. "Are you angry at Vicki because she didn't stop the library being shut down? Or are you upset with her because of how she handled everything?"

"Both," April grumbled. She ran her thumb over the chip on the rim of her mug. "I guess I can't blame her for what happened to the library."

"What about everything else? If it wasn't for everything with the library, would you forgive her for it?"

April crossed her arms. "I don't know."

"Just think about it," Eliza said.

"I will."

April didn't leave Eliza's house until late at night. By then, April just wanted to curl up in bed and cry. Her oldest friend was leaving. She had lost her library. She had lost her sanctuary.

But what hurt more than everything else was that she had lost Vicki.

CHAPTER TWENTY-THREE

*A*pril spent the next few days feeling lost and listless. With the library shut down, she had nothing to do with her time. At the very least, Lexi was in the same position. They'd met up for lunch earlier in the day and spent the afternoon hanging out.

But now, April was alone in her apartment, with nothing to distract her from her worries. She spent the whole evening reading, but only managed to get through a single chapter. Her mind kept returning to Vicki.

April put her book down with a sigh. As usual, Eliza was right. April was blaming Vicki for everything that had happened with the library. But it wasn't her fault. And this wasn't the first time April had blamed Vicki for things she had no control over. April had been unkind to her from the start when they first found out they were working against each other. And all the while, Vicki had put up with April's misdirected anger with barely a word.

April's phone buzzed on the coffee table. It was a message from Mel, the woman she'd met at the masquerade ball that night with Vicki. They'd exchanged a few texts about Mel's workplace offering legal resources to the library's patrons, but they hadn't gotten around to working out the details. It didn't matter now that the library was closed.

April opened the message.

I heard the good news about the library. I'm glad everything worked out in the end. We should meet up and discuss getting that partnership up and running.

Clearly, Mel had gotten her wires crossed somewhere. April typed out a reply.

I don't know what you've heard, but the library has been shut down.

What about the new site? Vanessa said that everything with the King Street building has been finalized.

King Street? That was definitely a mistake. King Street was right in the middle of West Heights, where properties now cost a fortune. And what did Mel's girlfriend have to do with anything?

I have no idea what you're talking about. I haven't heard anything about a new site, April sent back.

Mel took a while to respond. *Aren't you working with Vicki on this?*

Vicki. April's stomach fluttered. She began to type out a reply, then gave up and called Mel instead.

"What's going on, Mel?" April said. "What have you heard about the library?"

"You really don't know?" Mel asked. "I thought you were behind all this."

"Behind what?" April rubbed her temples. "Can you just tell me what you know?"

"Well, a couple of weeks ago, Vicki approached Vanessa about helping fund a new location for the library. Vanessa agreed—with a little prodding from me. Vicki updated her today that everything had been finalized."

That didn't make any sense. Vicki wasn't working on the project anymore. What the hell was she up to?

"Are you there?" Mel asked.

"Yeah. It's just, this is all news to me," April said.

"Seriously? I thought you and Vicki were doing this together. Actually, I thought it was all you since Vicki is, well, Vicki. She isn't exactly the most generous person."

"I haven't spoken to her in a while, actually," April admitted.

"Oh, sorry," Mel said. "I didn't know the two of you broke up."

April didn't bother correcting her. "Did Vicki say anything else about this?"

"That's all I know."

"This doesn't make any sense. Why would Vicki do something like that and not tell me about it?"

"That's way above my pay grade," Mel said. "You'll have to ask Vicki that."

"Thanks, Mel," April said.

"No problem. Good luck with Vicki."

April hung up and stared at her phone. Mel was right. If April wanted to get to the bottom of this, she had to go straight to the source.

April dialed Vicki's number and paced next to the couch, waiting for Vicki to pick up. It seemed to take an eternity. She was about to lose her nerve when Vicki finally answered.

"April?" Vicki said.

April didn't give her a chance to say hello. "Mel told me about King Street. What the hell is going on, Victoria?"

There was silence at the end of the line.

"Let me show you," Vicki finally said. "Meet me at the north end of King Street tomorrow morning."

"I'm not waiting until tomorrow," April said. "I want to know *now*."

"All right. Meet me on King Street in an hour?"

By the time April arrived on King Street, the sun had set. She was early, but Vicki was already there, standing under a streetlight waiting for her.

April's heart skipped a beat. That part of her that went weak every time she laid eyes on Vicki was still there, no matter how hard April tried to ignore it.

Spotting April, Vicki flashed her that devastatingly sexy smile. "Hi, April."

A storm of emotions erupted inside April. *"Hi, April? That's all you have to say? I hear nothing from you in more than a week, and now I'm finding out from Mel that you've found a new site for the library? What did you do?"*

"Looks like the secret is out." Vicki cocked her head toward the building next to them. "This is it. The new library."

"What?" April looked at the building before them. The beautiful sandstone construction had to be a hundred years old, but it was in perfect condition. It was huge, at least twice the size of the old Oakmont Street Library. "You're saying that this is the new library?" April asked.

Vicki nodded. "It's all yours."

"But… how? There's no way Oasis would pay for something like this. And you're not even working on the Oakmont Street project anymore."

"I'm not. After everything that happened, I decided I was too close to it all, so I passed the lead to someone else. Oasis doesn't have anything to do with this."

"Then who did this? You?"

"Not just me," Vicki said. "I contributed, but there's no way I could afford this by myself. I had help."

"From who?" April asked.

"My friends. Remember all those 'rich snobs' you met at the ball? I convinced them to donate funds toward a new library. Of course, even with help, I couldn't get enough money to buy a place like this. It's worth millions. Luckily, Camilla owns several properties in the area. I convinced her to sell this one to the library at an outrageously low price."

April gaped at the building. "I can't believe it. It's perfect."

Vicki brandished a key. "Want to take a look inside?"

April turned back to Vicki. She had so many things she wanted to say, so many things she wanted to hear Vicki say. And her heart kept beating faster and faster.

But she just nodded. "Sure."

The two of them climbed the stairs leading up to the front of the building.

"You're going to love it." Vicki struggled with the lock on the ornate wooden doors. "It used to be a museum, but it was shut down in the 80s and the building fell into disrepair. Camilla's family bought it decades ago, but they haven't done anything with it. It's been sitting here, empty, all these years."

Vicki finally managed to unlock the doors. She flung them open.

April's jaw dropped. "Wow."

The grand old building was just as beautiful on the inside as it was on the outside. It had high ceilings covered in mosaic tiles and marble floors. And it was huge. Their footsteps echoed through the vast space as they walked.

"This is amazing," April said.

There was so much space. The entrance hall had countless rooms coming off it, some large, some small, and there was a second floor. They wouldn't have to worry about having to adjust the schedule so that AA meetings and book clubs wouldn't fall at the same time. They could add new activities too, and they could even hold events here. There was so much room for the library to grow. Ideas started forming in April's mind. She couldn't wait to tell Lexi.

"As you can see, it needs renovations," Vicki said. "The money from your fundraiser should cover most of it. I can put you in touch with some contractors who will do the work at a discount."

April turned to Vicki. "Why didn't you tell me about this?"

"Well, the last time we spoke, you weren't exactly happy with me."

Right. In her excitement about the library, April had forgotten about everything. "Is this some sort of grand gesture to win me back? Were you planning to show up on my doorstep and announce that you'd swooped in to save the library?"

"No, it's not," Vicki said. "Although, if this does win you back, it's a bonus."

April put her hands on her hips. "Victoria!"

"I'm kidding, of course." Vicki held up her hands. "I started this before we even had that fight. I would have told you about what I was doing, but I didn't want to get your hopes up in case it didn't work out."

"Why?" April asked. "Why did you do this if it wasn't to impress me?"

"I did it because you made an impression on me. You're always talking about the library, and the community, and how much it all means to you. You made me realize how important a place like the library is to the people of West Heights. I knew from the start that I was never going to be able to save the Oakmont Street building, so I did the next best thing. I gave the Oakmont Street Library a new home."

April stared at her. "How long have you been working on this?"

"I started setting things in motion a few days after the ball," Vicki replied. "That night, I told you that the people in that room were the people who have the power to effect change. I was speaking about the long term, but it made me realize that I could make a difference right now."

"All this time, I thought you didn't care."

"I didn't, not until recently. I've been wandering through the world, living for superficial pleasures, not thinking or caring about anyone else. Then you came along and spoiled all that." Vicki gave her a faint smile. "You've changed me. You make me a better person."

"Vicki…"

"I didn't do this to get you back," Vicki said. "But that doesn't mean I don't want you back. And I want you to know that I'm sorry for everything. I'm sorry I didn't tell you that Oasis was planning to restart the development project. I'm sorry I wasn't there for you when you needed me. I'll never do anything like that again. I'll never do anything to hurt you again."

April's heart skittered in her chest. "I need to apologize too," she said. "For as long as we've known each other, I've treated you so badly. I was angry about everything, and I took it out on you, and I'm sorry. It wasn't fair. You never deserved it, but you stuck around anyway."

"Of course I did," Vicki said. She took April's hands. "I love you, April."

"I…" April took a calming breath. "I love you too."

Before she knew what she was doing, April's lips were on Vicki's in an urgent, demanding kiss.

CHAPTER TWENTY-FOUR

*T*he week that followed passed by in a blur. It would be months before the King Street Library could open its doors, but April had so much to do. Scheduling renovations. Chasing up donations. Organizing a large-scale fundraising campaign so that the library could expand its services. April barely had a chance to see Vicki at all.

Finally, on Friday evening, April paid a visit to Vicki's apartment. As soon as she arrived, Vicki dragged her inside, kissing her fervently. After a few minutes of this, they sat down in the living room with a drink. Sebastian leaped up to perch on the arm of the couch next to April.

Vicki smiled. "I think he likes you."

"About time," April reached out to stroke his fur. He purred and closed his eyes.

"I received some news at work today," Vicki said. "About the promotion."

April's stomach swam. She'd forgotten all about it. The job on offer was at Oasis' head office in Boston.

"I didn't even know I was still being considered for the position," Vicki continued. "The board wasn't too impressed with me after I gave up the Oakmont Street project. Not to mention the fact that I'm in a relationship with the woman who's been standing in the way of the project."

"Did you get the promotion?" April asked.

"I did." Vicki leaned back and crossed her legs. "They said despite my recent 'indiscretions,' I'm still the best candidate for the job."

"Oh." April avoided Vicki's gaze. "That's great."

"Hey." Vicki took April's hand. "I said no, of course."

"But you wanted this so badly. Your career is so important to you."

"It is. But you're even more important to me. After everything we've been through, I'd be an idiot to throw this relationship away."

"We could move to Boston together," April said. "I could get a job there."

"No," Vicki said. "I couldn't live with myself if I took you away from West Heights. This place is your home."

Relief washed over April. Vicki was right. April could never leave West Heights, let alone the city. At least, not right now.

"Besides, I don't need a promotion to prove myself. I don't need to prove myself to anyone. I know what I'm capable of, and so does everyone who's important to me." Vicki squeezed April's hand. "I didn't realize it until I ran into my parents at that charity ball, but my obsession with my career only meant that my life was still being dictated by my family's expectations, even if I was going against what they wanted for me. By choosing to follow my heart instead, I feel like I'm finally free of them, in a way."

"As long as you're doing what makes you happy," April said.

"I am. Besides, I've been thinking about finding a new job."

"Really? You've been at Oasis for so long."

"That's why I need a change," Vicki said. "I only took the job at Oasis because no one else would hire me. With all the experience I have now, my options have opened up. I've been putting out feelers, and I already have a few tentative offers."

"That's great," April said.

"What about you? How's the new library shaping up?"

"Everything's finally starting to come together. Once renovations are up and running, I'm going to have so much free time." April stretched out and sank into the couch. "I have no idea what I'm going to do with myself."

"I have a few ideas." Vicki took April's glass from her hand and placed it on the table next to them, then she leaned in and pressed her lips to April's.

April deepened the kiss. Her hands roamed down Vicki's body, feeling the slight swell of her slender hips, her flat stomach, her soft breasts. Vicki grasped at April's curves with double the intensity. April let out a blissful hum. Every time Vicki touched her, it set off fireworks inside.

Vicki broke away. "I want you in the bedroom and out of those clothes."

"Yes, ma'am." April jumped up from the couch.

They made their way to the bedroom where April

slipped off her jacket and dress. Vicki kicked off her jeans but left her blouse on.

Vicki gestured toward April's bra and panties. "Take those off too. Then stand by the bed and wait for me."

April stripped off her underwear and sat on the bed. She crossed her legs and leaned back on her elbows, watching Vicki's growing irritation.

Vicki's eyes rolled down the length of April's naked body. "You just can't help but test me, can you?"

April grinned.

Vicki shook her head. "You're on very thin ice." She went to the chest at the end of her bed and sifted through it. Finally, she pulled out the red strap-on.

The ache in April's core flared up, her body remembering the last time Vicki had used that strap-on. She waited eagerly for Vicki to step into it.

Instead, Vicki held it out to her. "Put this on."

April stared at her. "You want me to wear that?"

"Is there a problem?" Vicki asked.

"No." April was experienced enough with both ends of a strap-on. She was simply surprised. "Doesn't this spoil your big, bad Domme act?"

Vicki's lips curled up in a smile. "I assure you, I have every intention of topping you, even with you wearing that." She glanced pointedly at her closet door.

"Oh, really?" April said. "And how are you going to do that?"

"That's the second time you've ignored my instructions." Vicki held out the strap-on again. "Put this on, *now*."

April scowled at her but took the strap-on from her hands. Once April had it fastened around her hips, Vicki walked over to the closet at the side of the room and pulled the doors open.

Excitement welled up inside April. There were so many things in that closet that Vicki could use on her. Ropes. Whips. Gags. Not to mention all the things April didn't even recognize.

"Since you keep ignoring my instructions, I'm going to make it a little easier for you to follow them." Vicki scanned everything on display, her eyes lingering on some loops of rope and some handcuffs hanging from hooks. Finally, she opened a drawer beneath them and took out four pairs of leather cuffs.

April's eyes widened. *Four pairs?* April had been cuffed to a bed before, but not like this.

Vicki brought the cuffs over to the bed and dropped them next to April. "Lie down and put your arms up." As soon as April obeyed, Vicki began to cuff her wrists to the bedposts.

"You know," April said. "For someone who said she doesn't need tools, you sure use a lot of them."

Vicki spanked April on the side of the ass, hard. April squealed and began to wriggle in her bonds.

"Hold still," Vicki commanded.

April stopped moving. Vicki's heavy stare made one thing clear—she wasn't playing around anymore.

Vicki finished cuffing April's ankles. April tested her restraints. They didn't budge. With her limbs stretched to their limits, she was completely immobilized. And with Vicki still in her blouse and panties, April felt exposed in comparison.

Once again, April was at Vicki's mercy. It was clear from

the look on Vicki's face that she was going to take advantage of that fact.

Goosebumps sprouted on April's bare skin. Her heart began to race. Vicki didn't actually scare her. It was all a game. But April's body didn't know that. Her body didn't know she was safe. And her body's primal reaction to physical danger was to set all her senses on high alert. It only heightened her arousal.

"You're going to lie there, perfectly still," Vicki said. "Don't move, don't make a sound, until I give you permission. Understand?"

April nodded. Bound as she was, she could barely move anyway.

Vicki slipped out of her panties and crawled onto the bed. Straddling April's body, Vicki began to toy with her. She traced lines all over April's skin with her fingertips, so lightly that it tickled. She drew her fingers down to April's nipples, then pinched them, then ran her tongue over them. She scratched her nails down the length of April's torso and up the insides of her thighs, leaving red stripes behind on her skin.

April trembled on the bed, overcome by it all. The feel of Vicki's moist, ravenous lips on her skin. The scent of her body, musky and sweet. The touch of Vicki's fingertips in sensitive places. She longed to cry out, to speak Vicki's name like it was something sacred, but she held everything back, remaining silent and still.

Just when April couldn't take anymore, Vicki slid down April's body, positioning herself above the strap-on protruding from the peak of April's thighs.

"Remember," Vicki said. "Don't move."

She wrapped her fist around the strap-on, guiding it between her legs, and lowered herself onto it. She placed a hand on April's stomach to steady herself, her other hand flying up to her own head. Closing her eyes, she began to rock her hips.

April hissed. With every tiny movement Vicki made, the base of the strap-on pressed hard on April's clit, sending jolts of lightning through her. April desperately wanted to match Vicki's slow, deliberate motions. But Vicki had given her a command. So April lay there, bursting with need, using all her strength to keep herself from moving.

"God, this feels good." Vicki began to move faster, bouncing up and down. She slid her hands up to April's breasts, kneading them, and rolling the pads of her thumbs over April's peaked nipples.

April whimpered. The sight of Vicki above her, riding her like there was no tomorrow, made her throb inside. There was a faint sheen of sweat on Vicki's brow, and a wisp of her short hair had fallen across her forehead.

Vicki's head fell back. "Fuck me," she said. "You can yell, and scream, and moan. Go crazy."

That was the signal she'd been waiting for. April began to roll her hips, pushing her bound body to the limits of its motion, penetrating Vicki deeper. They got into a rhythm, rocking against each other in tandem. April pulled at her restraints. She'd never come while on this end of a strap-on before, but the pressure between her thighs was rising.

"I'm so close," Vicki said breathily. Thrusting and grinding feverishly, Vicki leaned down and smothered April's mouth with her own.

Suddenly, Vicki let out a cry, as an orgasm overtook her.

As Vicki convulsed on top of her, ecstasy surged deep within April's body, rolling through her in unrelenting waves.

Finally, Vicki stilled on top of her, her breath shuddering. "Fuck. That was…" She rolled onto her side next to April.

"Can you uncuff me now?" April asked.

Vicki ran her eyes along April's stretched out body. "I can," she replied. "Or I can leave you cuffed to the bed and spend the rest of the night playing with that exquisite body of yours."

"What do you plan to do with me?" April asked.

"If I told you, it would spoil the fun," Vicki said. "What do you say? I release you? Or I leave you on that bed and I have my way with you for the next few hours?"

April was torn between wanting to keep going and wanting to be free so she could hold Vicki in her arms and never let her go. The thrill of exploring dark, unknown delights with the woman she loved won out.

"I choose the second option," April said.

Vicki cupped April's cheeks and kissed her gently, then got up from the bed and walked over to the closet. She surveyed its contents.

"Now," Vicki said. "Where should I begin?"

EPILOGUE
VICKI

*V*icki stood in the entrance hall of the King Street Library, Camilla and Vanessa by her side, watching April make a speech from up on the landing of the staircase. It was the grand opening of the library, and April and Lexi had organized a huge gala event to raise even more funds.

April had taken Vicki's advice and had spent the last few months lobbying the city's policymakers. The room was packed with politicians and influential people. April had more than proven that she could go toe to toe with them.

"She's really something, isn't she?" Camilla said.

Vicki smiled. "She is."

Vicki had to admit, she'd underestimated April when they met. She'd had an inkling that there was more to April than the feisty temptress she'd taken home from Sapphire that night. What she wasn't expecting was this radiant firecracker of a woman who fought hard for what she believed in and constantly drove Vicki crazy.

Vicki wouldn't have it any other way.

"I never thought I'd live to see this day," Vanessa said. "Victoria Blake, tamed and tied down."

Vicki rolled her eyes. "Like you can talk. You and Mel moved in together after, what, a few months? She has you thoroughly domesticated."

"Melanie was very impressed with what you did for the library. Keep this up, and she might actually start to *like* you."

Camilla gave them both a stern glare. "Will the two of you stop bickering?" She downed the last of her wine. "I swear, every time we get together, I feel like I'm babysitting."

"Relax," Vicki said. "We're just messing around."

Vanessa gave Vicki a faint smile. "I *am* happy for you. Really."

"Oh? Does this mean you've finally dropped this grudge you've been holding against me?"

The truth was, she deserved Vanessa's animosity. Back then, Vicki hadn't known how serious Vanessa was about Mel, and she'd never intended to cause so much trouble. That was no excuse. Screwing up the relationship of one of her oldest friends had been a wake-up call for Vicki, one that had set her life on a less destructive path.

"I haven't decided yet," Vanessa said. "Although I've been enjoying watching you grovel, it's clear that you've changed your ways. I have to say, I'm impressed with what you've done for the library too."

"It wouldn't have been possible without both of you," Vicki said. "Thanks again. You've been very generous."

"I'm just doing my part for the city," Camilla replied. "Besides, April made an impression on me at that ball."

"She has that effect on people."

April's speech ended. The crowd broke out into applause. April stood there for a moment, glowing with pride, before descending the stairs.

"You'll have to bring April to the manor sometime," Camilla said. "It's been a while since you've visited."

"April would love that," Vicki replied.

"You too, Vanessa. Bring Mel along. And, if you come in the next month or so, you'll get to meet my guest."

"Your guest?" Vicki asked. "I'm intrigued."

"I think you'd like her," Camilla said, her eyes sparkling.

Before Vicki could question Camilla further, April approached them.

"We'll leave you two alone," Camilla said. She gave them a warm smile before wandering off with Vanessa.

Vicki wrapped her arms around April's waist. "You were incredible up there."

April grinned. "Thanks."

"Seriously, do you have any idea what an amazing woman you are?"

April wrapped her arms around Vicki's neck. "You may have told me once or twice."

Vicki drew April in for a kiss. She heard the flash of a camera going off.

"Caught in the act again," April said.

"I don't care if you don't," Vicki said.

"We better make sure they get a good picture."

April kissed Vicki, harder this time. Her fiery kisses still set Vicki alight. Right now, she wanted nothing more than to find an empty room and tear off that pretty, delicate dress April was wearing.

Vicki broke off the kiss before she could get too carried away.

April gazed around the room. "I just can't believe we pulled this off."

"It was all you," Vicki said.

"I couldn't have done it without you. And all those friends of yours."

"They only helped get things off the ground. You're the one who brought the new library to life. You're the reason that all these people are here tonight."

"About that," April said. "I've made my decision. I'm going to run for city council."

"That's great," Vicki said. "You're definitely going to win. Everyone in West Heights loves you for everything you've done with the library."

"You think so?"

"I know so. And you're destined for far bigger things. Who knows, maybe in a few years you'll be Mayor."

"Let's not get ahead of ourselves," April said. "I mean, I don't know anything about running for office. I'm going to need all the help I can get."

"I'll do whatever I can to support you," Vicki said. "And when you become a councilwoman, you can help me out with building permits."

Vicki had taken a job as CEO at a smaller property development company, one that was far more scrupulous than Oasis. It was a step up in terms of her career, but she had taken a pay cut. It was worth it.

"I'm pretty sure giving my girlfriend building permits would be an abuse of my position. Although it could be fun to have all that power over you. To have you at my mercy."

Her eyes twinkling, April stood on her toes to speak into Vicki's ear. "I could even make you beg."

Vicki narrowed her eyes. "You've been trying to push my buttons all day. And I don't like it."

April gave her a cheeky smile. "What are you going to do about it?"

"Oh, you're going to be in so much trouble when we get home."

With her arms still around April, Vicki couldn't help but notice the tiny shift in the other woman's body at her words, and the hint of scarlet that spread up her cheeks.

"I can't wait." April kissed Vicki gently and took her hand. "Come on. Let's go mingle."

ABOUT THE AUTHOR

Anna Stone is the bestselling author of the Irresistibly Bound series. Her sizzling romance novels feature strong, complex, passionate women who love women. In every one of her books, you'll find off-the-charts heat and a guaranteed happily ever after.
Anna lives on the sunny east coast of Australia. When she isn't writing, she can usually be found with a coffee in one hand and a book in the other.

Visit annastoneauthor.com for information on her books and to sign up for her newsletter.

 facebook.com/AnnaStoneRomance
twitter.com/AnnaStoneAuthor

Made in the USA
Columbia, SC
10 September 2022

66916170R00140